Two Pharoahs
Hatshepsut and Tuthmose III

by

Philip R. Clark

authorHOUSE®

AuthorHouse™
1663 Liberty Drive, Suite 200
Bloomington, IN 47403
www.authorhouse.com
Phone: 1-800-839-8640

© 2007 Philip R. Clark. All rights reserved.
No part of this book may be reproduced, stored in
a retrieval system, or transmitted by any means
without the written permission of the author.
First published by AuthorHouse

Printed in the United States of America   12/10/2007
Bloomington, Indiana
This book is printed on acid-free paper.
ISBN: 978-1-4343-4420-5 (sc)

TWO PHARAOHS
HATSHEPSUT AND TUTHMOSE III

A long time friend refused to read any of my novels and that his inclination was more to stories based on reality. Novels, of which I have written several., are based on something imaginary, figments of my imagination, thoughts gone astray, smoke and mirrors. So I was challenged by his attitude which sent me back to another project I had set aside some time ago. It is a novel set in a period, thirty-five centuries ago when a female Pharaoh HATSHEPSUT ruled over Egypt. As you would expect she had competitors, one of which was TUTHMOSE III and who was closely related to her. In fact he claimed that he was her nephew, or better yet he was her half nephew, the son of the pharaoh, TUTHMOSE II, who just happened to be married to HATSHEPSUT, and had TUTHMOSE III not with HATSHEPSUT, but with a 'harem' wife, ISIS. That would make HATSHEPSUT, his stepmother. However, she was the only, and favored daughter of a phraoah and his wife.the Queen. Tuthmose III's father was also a pharaoh, who also just happened to be HATSHEPSUT's: husband, who by the way also was her younger brother. Please don't be confused and just accept the idea that intermarriage and intrigues were quite common among the royalty in ancient Egypt. But that didn't slow them down or stop the competition as to who was the legitimate pharaoh. And to confuse matters more he may even have been married to Hatshepsut's daughter.

The verbiage will not be as spoken in that time, but will be in the contemporary mode. The customs of the time will more closely resemble those as we know them today with definite variations. In spite of the vast separation in time many things done by those at the time resemble what is done today, with volitility. I hope that this will be adequate inducement to read a book about something that just could interest any reader. In any event, I dedicate the book to my brother-in-law, Edward L. Rimpau, Jr. and hope that this one will encourage him to read a novel. PRC. Author

TALE OF TWO PHARAOHS
Philip R. Clark
FOREWORD

We have all heard of Cleopatra, a Queen and a Pharaoh in ancient Egypt, who was able to turn the heads of both Julius Caesar and Mark Antony with her remarkable beauty, even to having a son, by Caesar, naming him Caesarion. She surely facinated the two of them, and lots of Rome, as has been reputed, with her charms. However she was unable to use them on Octavian, who defeated her Egyptian forces and those of her lover, Mark Antony in the naval battle at Actium. Defeated and in despair, she resorted to suicide as she is reputed to have allowed a venomous asp to bite her, thereby ending her life. Cleopatra was the last pharaoh in Egypt. Oddly enough Hatshepsut was a woman also, an anonmoly as she joined a small cadre of women rulers, who with those classical male pharaohs and who ruled in Egypt during the dynastic periods which all together lasted for over eighteen hundred years.

However, little has been written outside of scholarly and historical treatises regarding one of Cleopatra's predecessors, Ma'at-ka-Ra Hatshepsut, or Hatshepsut, as she is known, one of a few female pharaohs of Egypt and one of the more successful ones. This is an imaginary piece by the author, a novel about her and her times, her trials and the tribulations that drove her, a beautiful woman, to wear a pharonic false beard, and other ornamentations normally worn by male pharaohs, to have images inscribed of her which would depict her dainty body with bulging muscles, even a male-like appearance all to satisfy her detractors of which there were many. But all were not detractors, there were also suitors---------.

The records, as written by esteemed Egyptologists are thoroughly mixed and the only real fact, will you, is that her father was the popular Tuthmose 1, and her mother has been called by many differents names, but for our story we selected only one of them, Ahmose. So reader please bear with me as I am not an Egyptologist, only a lay person who will, in part, concoct a story derived from the mix of information available through multiple sources that I was able to use. If for any reason one of the expert Egyptologist take issue with what I have written, I will tell him that this is a novel, some or all of which may, just may be true.

I seriously doubt that her fellow Egyptians called her Ma'at-ka-Ra Hatshepsut, as the last part of the name is how she is known in the history books. The total name is only seven syllables, but it is a mouthful, so for the book's sake and to rest my typing fingers, I, with your permission, will resort to referring to her as Ma'at-ka-Ra, instead of Ma'at-ka –Ra Hatshepsut *etc, at least for the start of my novel,* but will frequently refer to her by the name she is best known, or Hatshepsut. That way we do not lose her whole name by calling her Nancy or Jean or something like that. However some clarification is due to explain the longer version of her name as it was given to her by her father, Tuthmose I, a Pharaoh and thereby designated as a god. Her mother was Ahmose, also of the royal blood line, a necessity that the royal blood line come from the mother thus Ahmose may have been and possibly was even closely related to her own husband, Tuthmose I.

But to further explain Hatshepsut full name, *Ma'at* stands for *truth*, ka means *soul* and *ra* is the Sun God. Put together it means *Truth* is the *Soul* of the *Sun God.* And *Hatshepsut* means *Foremost of Noble Women.* All symbolic, nothing like Nancy or Jean, but we really don't know where those names, contemporary at the time, really came from anyway. However, to maintain some semblence of accuracy, the actual names will be alternately used.

And that was her and by no means the end of the story. It turns out that she had a stepson Tuthmose III who almost from the start of his life was destined to be a pharaoh. This was a goal that he pursued with great vigor and with the assistance of his mother, Isis and others actually was able to achieve the 'godly' throne of the pharaoh and proved after all the skullduggery that he would turn out to be one the best of all the pharaohs.

NOTE: Contemporary names were used in describing or referring to geographical locations instead of the antiquated or old Egyptian names. Examples: Aswan was called *Abu*. Menphis was called *Hwt-ka-Ptah* and Egypt itself was called *Kemet*.

A glossary of terms, names and definitios follows to clarify all others.

GLOSSARY OF NAMES, TERMS AND LOCATIONS

Ahmose	Queen, wife of Tuthmose I mother of Hatshepsut
Akhohop	Palace guard, loyalist, Senemut faction
Akhom	Scribe and Senemut's Assistant pretended conspirator
Amenhotep	Tuthmose III Son and Successor
Amisi	Tuthmose III's minor wife. literal meaning "Flower"
Anenemes	Son of Tuthmose I and Ahmose, deceased
Antyu	Incense treasured by Egyptians and imported fromLand of Punt
Aty	Queen Land of Punt

Amon-Ra	Thebian god who took a human form to impregnate Ahmose
Anenemes	Son of Ahmose and Tuthmose I, deceased
Atum	God, creator of the world. Egyptian
Byblos	Seaport and ancient city in Syria (Lebanon)
Deir el-Bahri	Part of the Valley of Kings
Dimasqu	Damascus, Syria
Djahy	Southern portion of Syria
Djeserit	Genaral Neti's wife, relative of Harere, Akhom's wife
Djeser-Djeseru	"Holiest of Holies", Hatshepsut's Mortuary Temple
Electrum	gold and silver alloy, treasured by the Egyptians
Great Sea	Mediterranean Sea
HaremWife	Alternative wife, not the primary wife, probably not royal
Harere	Akhom's wife
Hurrians	Indo-Aryan people from Northeast Mesopotamia (Iraq)

Hyksos	An Asian, possibly Indo-Semetic people who invaded Egypt and ruled for 100 years in period from 1648-1540 BC
Ineni	Egptian Architect and builder
Isis	Godess associated with fertility
Isis	Minor wife to Tuthmose II, mother of Tuthmose III
Karnak	Iper-Isut Thebian Location of sacred tombs, modern Luxor
Khasekhem	Son of Isis and Menes
Khepresh	War crown worn by Pharaohs
Khnoum	God, the divine potter
Land of Punt	In present day Somalia and part of Sudan
Ma'at-ka-Ra	Another name for Hatshepsut
Megiddo	Tel Megiddo in present day Israel. Canaanite fortress
Menes	Egyptian general and conspirator
Merytra	Merytra-Hatshepsut, Thuthmose III royal wife, mother of pharaoh Amentohop II
Meti	Palace guard, Amisi's lover

Mitanni	Hurrian kingdom in ancient Mesopotamia (Iraq)
Montnofrit	Commoner, son of Tuthmose I
Mutnofret	Minor wife Tuthmose I, mother of Tuthmose II
Neferure	Hapshepsut's daughter with Senenmut, claimed by Tuthmose II
Nehsi	Nubian General
Nemes	Pharonic crown, worn over head, a section with stripes going down the back
Neti	Egyptian general and conspirator
Nome	Egyptian admistrative equivalent to a county in the United States
Osiris	God of the underworld, Egyptian
Parakin	King of Land of Punt
Phoenicia(n)	Includes present day Syria, as it did in history, but historically includes all of the Levant, ie: Palestine, Israel, Lebanon and as far East to include parts of Mesopotamia.
Quesir	Egyptian Port on the Red Sea
Ra	Famous and one of the most important of Egyptian dieties

Senenmut	Hapshepsut's tutor, confidant, Chancellor, Steward and lover
Stele	honorary inscription carved in stone or a pillar
Vizier	Prime Minister, most valued advisor to Pharaoh
Wadjimose	Son of Ahmose and Tuthmose I, deceased

CHAPTER ONE
A Beginning

The cries that came from the adjacent chambers alarmed Tuthmose I, as he had heard those sounds before, twice before when Wadjimose and Anenemes were born, but these seemed more urgent, louder, and as his wife Queen Ahmose pleaded with the gods for some relief, even death, anything to be delivered of the pain she was encoutering. She loudly blamed her Pharaoh husband for his earlier participation in the act which brought on such pain. But soon there was the cry from a baby and all became quiet, except for the nonsensical babblings of the royal physicians and attendants. Tuthmose I could stand it no longer and entered the queen's chamber as the attendants were cleaning up the new arrival. He went over and looked at the new born.

"A girl/" A little hesitation "Not a boy?" After looking, a sign of dismay on his face. They had two boys before, but they did not survive , but the birth of a boy was most important in these troubled times. The Eighteenth Dynasty needed to have a new leader in-waiting to be able to sustain itself, a son, a boy who would in time develop into another pharaoh, no mean position.

"A beautiful girl, someday you will be very proud of her, if not today" replied the physician, prophetically. Tuthmose went to the Queen, now somewhat composed as the attendants cared for her immediate personal needs.

"I'm sorry my Tuthmose, we will try again" her voice husky after all of the cries for divine assistance during the delivery ordeal, "and I fervently prayed to the godess Isis, for a boy as I knew that you wanted one so badly, but----" her voice trailing off followed by a sob.

"Don't worry about that now. Just rest. You did your best. Yes we will try again."

A group of priests from the temple of Amun, also for their own personal reasons, were concerned with the duration of the dynasty, confided with Tuthmose I and carefully cautioned the pharaoh that it was most important that he somehow be sure to produce an heir. Usurpers abounded, and only the enduring popularity of the pharaoh prevented a revolt from well organized opportunists.

Tuthmose heeded the advice being given him he and Ahmose prayed fervently to Ra for a son and heir. And as time passed by and when they were able, they did try again, and again and soon she was pregnant, once more. Years had passed though, and although there had been two boys before Hatshepsut, but they did not live.

Two Pharoahs

Only problem was that the anxious pharaoh, trying to hedge his bets, in the twenty-first century vernacular, consorted with one of his minor wives, Mutnofret, and she presented him a son and therefore an heir. He was named Tuthmose II. The temple priests were momentarily relieved and satisfied, as their very existence was tied into the orderly continuance of the present dynasty.

In addition to this 'arrangement' Tuthmose had another affair with a commoner and from that relationship came another son, Moutnofrit, who because of his mother, would not be eligible to become Pharaoh. That birth, although a son, unfortunately by a mother, who was a commoner, thereby disqualifying him. Afterall she was a 'harem' wife and not one of 'royal' blood.

CHAPTER TWO

As Ma'at-ka-Ra and her younger brother matured and their parents aged a minor rivalry grew between them. The pharaoh was able to ascertain early that Hatshepsut possessed those qualities to be an effective ruler, whereas Tuthmose II seemed to lack those necessary for a competent pharoah. Unfortunately he was suffering from some infirmity which affected his skin. Consequently he spent most of his time with his mother, whereas his older sister, Hatshepsut, became the pharaoh's constant companion and when she could, she asked questions about matters of state, even made welcome suggestions

As Hatshepsut grew up in her father's shadow she early became his favorite and he wisely began to groom her for a leadership position. His intentions were fatherly and welcome by Ma'at-ka-Ra Hatshepsut with no apparent ulterior motivation by either of them. The more he had his beautiful daughter around him the better he liked it and as at the same time it was giving his daughter some semblence of what it takes to be a ruler. He worshipped the beautiful princess as she began to mature "So much like her mother" as he looked upward to the heavens and gave thanks to the gods.

However as time went by it was definitely evident to Tuthmose I that his Ma'at-ka-Ra's junior brother. Tuthmose II seemed ill fit, both mentally and physically, to assume the effective role of a pharaoh. And to avoid anyone from contesting his authority and make it appear more legal they, their children, brother and sister, were married. This was an acceptable practice and quite common and not an unusual custom in those times, especially among Egptian royalty. This pleased his chief vizier as well as the priestly class all of which were uneasy at the possibility of a revolt and a possible dynastic change. At the time both Hapshetsut and Tuthmose II were quite young and the Pharaoh, Tuthmose I was still ensconsed as the active and very popular Pharaoh

The Twenty-First Century reader may be a little confused by the marriage between a young sister and a younger brother . It probably wasn't a marriage in the same sense as we understand it. It wasn't a marriage with all of the romantic trappings we expect and see. As it turns out they were not even fond of each other, she was reported that she was even repulsed by him. Obviously, it was a marriage of convenience and to assure the continuance of the throne and thereby the dynasty, and save it from any possible usurpers or people with any alternative dynastic asperations. There was a great deal of competition for the position of Pharaoh in ancient Egypt, something not necessarily unusual in today's world. There was no moral compunction about this sort of thing in a lot of ancient civilizations. But what happened after this brings additional interest to this story. Intrigue and all of the accoutrements of power seeking appear in ways that would rival many lesser situations that occur in present days contemporary politics.

He, Tuthmose I, showed great interest in his inquisitive daughter, and at the same time was able to see the flagging qualities in his son and heir, Tuthmose II. In hopes of adding to her authoritative mastery, he assigned Senenmut, a commoner, with special skills, to the role of special tutor for his intelligent and capable daughter in hopes of adding to her authoritarian skills. Also he appointed her co-regent to Tuthmose II, thereby enhancing her potential position of authority which would with certainty come later.

Senenmut was very young, not much older than Ma'at-ka-Ra and fortunately very talented in matters of construction as well as governance. His family had been active as advisors to the Dynasties and he, being a good student, had little difficulty amassing this knowledge to his advantage. He eventually was given the title of royal steward, a noteworthy position enhancing his position in the court and with Hatshepsut.

He taught Ma'at-ka-Ra many things and found her to be an apt student and was actually amazed as to how well and quickly she learned the fundamentals of governance as he knew them. He was even more amazed how she, a female, a young woman, was as interested in matters related to his great love of building and architecture. Many monuments would later be commissioned by her after she became Queen/Pharaoh , some time later.

Two Pharoahs

Their relationship became quite close and Hatshepsut became actually closer to Senemut than she was to her husband, Tuthmose II. However no one seemed to mind or be concerned about the almost intimate relationship.

At the same time the connection between Tuthmose II and Hatshepsut was strained and their personal interaction cool at minimum. It probably was brought about by the attention paid Ma'at-ka-Ra by their father, the pharaoh. Also he was resentful of her physical appearance which was quite beautiful, making her the favorite of the court, especially with the men. Whereas his physical appearance was not helped by the obvious skin disease, some of which was probably caused by his attention to having a traditional smooth face necessitated by the removal of facial hair by plucking it from his face, hair by hair.

For his own Tuthmose II found his own solace, not with his wife, but with a minor wife, one of royal blood, Isis, who eventually bore him a son, Tuthmose III, and a new problem was created for the ruling couple, even though Tuthmose III was quite junior to Hatshepsut and her husband, the father, it became a nuisance particlarily for Ma'at-ka-Ra Hatshepsut, Queen/Regent as she later ascended the throne of Pharaoh and began to exercise more power. There were potential usurpers busily doing whatever they could to replace the female pharaoh-elect with one more to their liking.

No ordinary person, besides her authorative bearing, as she began to display great, but dainty physical beauty. This was further enhanced by the proper application of make up especially mascara around her deep green eyes.

Philip R. Clark

And as she grew in stature these physical attributes grew more alluring, her ample breasts clearly visible through the flimsy gowns of the day. However those who dared to look lasciviously at the beautiful woman did so through veiled eyes and at their peril. This apparenly did not apply to Senenmut, as the two of them became almost insepareable.

And when at one time, their bodies so close to each other, this very close proximity, one to the other, led to the inevitable. They were alone and Senenmut found himself unable to contain himself, first their hands touched, not the first time, and he took her hand in his and held it for some time as their eyes met, he started to pull away, and she stopped him, placing his hand on her breast.

He could feel her nipple grow hard and she took his other hand on her other breast, her warm breath now quite close to him. Senenmut knew that he dangerously close to her and she edged even closer, an uncomfortable urge came over him. He wanted to reach her, embrace her, but he knew that he was entering forbidden territory. All would be lost, possibly his life, if he went further. "Your husband, the Pharaoh will have my head."

"Don't you worry, my love. My father would not be surprised and would approve of it, albeit reluctantly. Tuthmose II has no desire for me, he never enters my bed and that is the way we have planned it. Besides he lays with that Isis as much as he can."

She reached for the other one of his hands and vigorously messaged her breast, moving his hand down to her stomach. His sense of desire for this young princess was

Two Pharoahs

becoming overpowering, when suddenly Hatshepsut took his face in both if her hands and kissed him full on his lips, a long kiss.

She then rose, making sure that none of attendants were present as she led him into her chamber, disrobed in front of him and beckoned him to follow her example.

"I love you, Senenmut, my glorious prince" as they both tried to catch their breaths after lustrous moments of ecstacy for the two of them.

"I love you too, Ma'at-ka-Ra, and have ever since you were a little one and your father, the Pharaoh, the great Tuthmose I, assigned me to be your tutor. But what will your husband think, and do, if this ever comes out?"

Still on the subject of concern in part for her personal safety, as well as his own "What of your husband?"

"Tuthmos II, he is my younger brother, as my husband, is a farce. Have you looked at him? His skin? He is quite repulsive to me. We have never slept in the same bed and will not. Neither of us have any desire to have it any other way.And as I have said he has his hands full with Isis. We all know it was a dynastic decision. So, my love, we are quite safe. I would do nothing to imperil you, especially you."And they fell into each other's arms and sleep overtook Hatshepsut. Senenmut, however, remained awake, feigning sleep, but awake all the same, and concerned about what had just occurred. He was truthful, that he, only a commoner, had overstepped his position with the princess, and that little good would come from it.

Philip R. Clark

Hatshepsut remained unconcerned and made a point of having Senenmut near at all times possible. Her husband was disinterested as he had little emotional feelings for his sister and like her realized that the rationale for the match was purely a dynastic decisiom. She was his beautiful sister and he loved her in just that way, as a sister.

But his sister was growing closer to Senenmut and although they tried to maintain an aura of normalcy. Only Tuthmose seemed to observe the familiarity being displayed by his wife and the commoner who had been appointed her tutor by his father Tuthmose I.. If tongues were wagging he did not hear them. He did need to have someone tell him, but he was sure that the relationship between the two had progressed into something more. She, although beautful and alluring, she was still his sister.

Then the unexpected and yet inevitable happened. She found out that she was pregnant and she was delirious with happiness and could hardly wait to tell her constant companion. Who, on his part, did not for the moment, share the joyous event. He was concerned about her brother, who, certainly at worst, might have his head for such an indiscretion. She assured him that nothing untoward would come of it from that source. In a jocular way she said "He might even take credit for it " to show all that his 'wife' had been compliant with his wishes and outwardly it would show."Don't worry, I'll handle it from this side"

When she began to show a little weight, and her stomach began to exhibit some unusual girth for the dainty princess, he confronted her and announced that the forthcoming baby will be accepted as his own and that they announce that it is so. Afterall he has his Isis and they have a future pharaoh, Tuthmose III.

"Now that you know," with trepidation "what of Senenmut? I love him so"

"You do not have to worry, my sister." And added "And, I might add, neither does he"

A girl was born and she was claimed by Tuthmose II and they named her Neferure, the name selected by the pharaoh.

CHAPTER THREE

In 1593 BC after a reasonably long period, for the times, Tuthmose I, the popular pharaoh who had accomplished much, especially in the combining Upper and Lower Egypt died after a reasonably lengthy reign where peace had been the rule of the day. And now for more turbulent times as the succession had been established and this resulted in the elevation of the young and inept Tuthmose II to the position of pharaoh and his wife, Ma'at-ka-Ra Hatshepsut being elevated to Queen/co-Regent as had been designated by her father.

However, Tuthmose III seeing the frailty of his disinterested father and through powerful surrogates arguing that the two parts of Egypt and the New Kingdom needed a stronger male leader to maintain the status quo, even though this assertion was made when he was quite young. This assumption was challenged by Tuthmose II and of course the queen-regent, Hatshepsut, who had assumed more power, than even her husband. A situation which incensed Tuthmose III and his promoters, mainly because he resented the power mantle whch Hatshepsut had assumed.

To be married toTuthmose II was far from ideal. He was her younger brother, a weakling and was beset with numerous illnesses from birth and eventually even died from a skin disease, probably leprosy, and within just a few years after he became the pharaoh. He was credited with the birth of one daughter, Neferure, although it is widely believed her lover, Senenmut was the father. One thing that Tuthmose I did was to have,at his demise,Tuthmose II and his Queen, Hatshepsut both assume the responsibiliteso of a pharaoh.

During Tuthmose'II reign, Hatshepsut fulfilled her father's wish and served as regent. However as Tuthmose II weakened she assumed a more prominent role or position much to the chagrin of Tuthmose III. Then as III thought that he would become Pharaoh, even though he still was very young, But, as Tuthmose II became sicker, and lingered on, thereby allowing his wife to assume more and more of the responsibilites of a leader-pharaoh.

At that time Hatshepsut proved she was masterful politician and an elegant stateswoman with adequate charisma to dissuade all challengers, including the considerableTuthmose III faction. She claimed that she had been handpicked by her father's god and in the temple were written the words of Khnoum, the divine potter, who had sculpted forms of the many gods' "I will make you first of all living creatures. You will rise as king of Upper and Lower Egypt, as your father, Amon. Who loves you did ordain"

And forthwith she added the story detailing the night when the Theban god Amon-Re impregnated her mother "Amon took the form of the noble king, Tuthmose and found the queen sleeping in her room. When the pleasant odors that emanated from him and he annonces his presence, she was awakened. He gave her his heart and showed himself in godlike splendor, When he approched the queen, she wept with joy at his strength and beauty and he gave his love."

Since the gods were called into the situation, momentarily, most of the challenges ended, with the exclusion of Tuthmose III. These propagandas worked well to cement Hatshepsut's position, but as Tuthmose III grew, her sovernity grew more tenuous. He not only resented his lack of authority, but no doubt harbored ill will toward his step-mother's consort, Senenmut. Senenmut, in turn, suggested the Tuthmose III be sent to the care of the priests of the temple to Amon, where certain disciplines could be taught. It was a suggestion which Hatshepsut heeded, much to Tuthmose III's disappointment and humiliation. The time he spent there was intended to bring peace to the distraught Queen, and did so, momentarily.

In the interlude an assortment of priests from the temple to Amon and her vizier all cautioned her that Tuthmose III with others were attempting to mount a coup to replace Hatshepsut before she actually assumed the official position of pharaoh.

When advised of this she said "None of them have the power to do that. The army is fully behind me and they too hope that there will be an heir as well, and that I will live long enough and remain capable of producing one."

Her relationship with Senenmut became even closer as she found an assortment of tasks for him and almost with each he was awarded a title. And during their long relationship he was awarded a total of ninety-three different titles surpassing all of those before him and all since.

She, for example, suggested that he erect two pointed obelisks adjacent to her father's monumental tomb at Karnak, one that would be high enough that it would be beseeching for him the blessings from Ra for his quick delivery to heaven after his death. These were carved at Aswan and floated down the Nile on boats manned by as many as a hundred oarsmen, per boat, mostly slaves from the areas south of Egypt.

Senenmut also announced that he had a proposal to build a monument tomb for Hatshepsut, "As you suggested," but had not yet selected the location. "What I have in mind is something rather large and it will occupy a large piece of land, maybe at Deir el-Bahri, in the Valley of the Kings. What do you think?"
"I await your final plans."

"Incidentally, Tuthmose III, said also that he would like to have the place set aside for his future burial location. Do you have a problem with that?"

"No, that is a little premature for him, he may never be a pharaoh.. I'll talk to him, and that will be the end of that."

CHAPTER .FOUR

This disappointed Tuthmose III, who seeing that his father was frail and inadequate to be pharaoh and the liklihood of his becoming pharaoh was getting more imminent as the days passed and that it was befitting that he plan for the future, which would include the ultimate selection of his burial site. But he had to reckon with Ma'at- ka-Ra Hatshepsut on this and other things as she propped up her husband and passed on to him whatever he had to be done or not done.

What no one had counted on was that Tuthmose II did not die, even though he remained quite ill and as he lingered on.and the intrigue began in earnest. Tuthmose II was deathly sick and the co-regent, Hatshepsut, began assuming all of the powers normally accorded only to the pharaoh, this, also, was to Tuthmose III's chagrin, who during this long illness, felt his entitlement was merely days if not moments away..

Further, Tuthmose III felt that he should be appointed pharaoh, especially if and when Tuthmose II passed away,

Two Pharoahs

which he did before too many more years went by. This made Tuthmose III even more insistant that he become pharaoh but he hadn't reckoned with his stepmother, so all of his desires were to no avail.

What was the position of Hatshepsut, already the queen-regent for Tuthmose II. She simply and masterfully took the position as the pharaoh. "You cannot be pharaoh, Hatshepsut, you are a woman, my step-mother and the position should go the remaing male heir, which I am."

"You are wrong, my son, there have been six other woman pharaohs and the records will assure you of that." To support her cause, she claimed the god Amon-Ra had spoken, "Welcome my sweet daughter, my favorite, the Kingdom of Upper and Lower Egypt, Ma'at-ka-ra Hatshepsut, thou are the King. Take possession of the lands."

Not to give up "But my stepmother, that was a long time ago. If you are not able to rule as a pharaoh should, then there will be others who will want to take over the power over both parts of Egypt."

"I have been told by my chancellor, Senenmut, that our dynasty has little to fear and I agree with him."

"You would and you have your special reasons.especially since I hear that he frequently occupies your bed."

"And that is my affair, and no affair of yours.." And she looked at Tuthmose III, eye to eye, until the man felt that he had lost the point entirely.

"I will not forget this, my step-mother." And he took those accompanying him and left.

Behind a column and out of sight from Tuthmose III, was Senenmut "You did well, my love. But you need to find somethimg for Tuthmose III to do to keep him busy and away from the center of the government. He does not wish you well, and I suspect that he will do something to remove you. What? I do not know, but something. I would be watchful at all times." Attested Senenmut, her long time tutor, lover and her Chancellor

"Let's not discuss this any more, there are just too many things that still have to be done to complete my coronation, which we should address as soon as posssible. Do you have any things to tell me about the celebration.?"

"To be sure to lend authenticity to the affair, I believe that we need to have the proper ornamentation accorded to a pharaoh, and these are being prepared as we speak."

"On second thought, why do we have to talk about things like this when we have other and better things to do" as she took Senenmut's hand and led him to her chamber. All of the attendants who were there were aware of her life with Senenmut, a relationship that had begun when her husband was alive and they were both quite young.

Senenmut was as handsome as his lady was beautiful. They made a handsome couple, and he seemed to be quite compatible with all of her plans to rule, as well as suggesting many of his own. He mentally towered over all of the other advisors that assisted her as queen/regent, and now that she planned to become pharaoh, he intended to become even more important to her. The fact that they had fallen in love with each other only made it all the better.

Two Pharoahs

He looked at her, her body now almost nude, and saw a woman, although still quite young, fully developed, her rounded firm breasts caused her outer attire to reveal everything.. Many of the men were known to see and talk about that feature if nothing else. To be verbose about her physical features could be quite dangerous, so many men would take a quick look and then lower their eyes. Her face was as beautiful as he had ever seen, her eyes were large, green and she used the special dressing to make her eyes more attractive. The substance with which she added colorations to the edges of her eyes had been brought back to Egypt on one of Egypt's trade missions to Land of Punt.. Then she included additional coloration to her cheeks, all of which just added to her natural beauty. He looked at her and thought and mummered, barely audible,"How will I turn this beauty into the severity of a Pharaoh?"

"Did you say something?" she asked him.

"No my lady, just thinking out loud." And they clasped each other, their bodies close.

"Senenmut, do you ever think that my illustrious stepson can bury his impatience and wait his time, that of course if I don't have a son?"

"I doubt it, my lady. He feels that his destiny is as a pharaoh. It has been ingrained in him by his mother, Isis, who sees an advantage in his becoming the pharaoh, So, he has constant pressure from that quarter so I don't see any significant change in him in the short term.

CHAPTER FIVE

Hatshepsut, accompanied by her chancellor, Senenmut. sought a place where they could have more privacy "What could you have in mind, my friend,?"

"It's about your stepson, Tuthmose III"

"What about him"

"Rumors abound. About-----"

"Rumors, about what?'

"Tuthmose III, I do not trust him, and neither should you, my lady. Despite the way he addresses you, beneath the surface he seethes with jealousy and thinks ill of you in spite of outward appearances."

"I am not worried about him and his sychophants." She reminded him of the words of the Oracle of Amun, stating that she was chosen by Amun with '*Welcome my sweet daughter, my favorite, the King of Upper and Lower Egypt, Maatkare, Hatshepsut, Thou art the Pharaoh, taking possession of the Two Lands'* and following that with another propaganda proclaimation speaking as if it were the words of her father, Tuthmose I saying '*This daughter of mine, Khnumetamun Hatshepsut-may she live- I have appointed as my successor upon my throne, she shall direct the people in every sphere of the palace, it is she indeed who will lead you. Obey her words, unite yourselves at her command*' All who heard this, among them royal nobles, other kings, dignataries, and the leaders of the people realized that this proclamation in effect elevated her to King, or Pharoah.

"Nevertheless, my lady, I would not expose my back to him."

"I can control him, as he swore allegiance to me when I told him that it was decided by the gods and that I should be the Pharoah and told him that that he should swear fealty to me."

"Nevertheless, he might try to do something untoward to you when you least expect it".

"What do you have in mind?"

"I don't know," concerned that he was talking about a man who would eventually be the pharaoh, "but as I told you before, he seethes with jealousy and anmosity, to say nothing about his ambition. And he's not above doing something rash. You must be ever careful.".

"What do you think if we encouraged him to organize and take a trade mission to, let me see, to the Land of Punt? Puntite trade missions have been here a number of times, but to my knowledge we've rarely reciprocated in kind. They have many products that are important to Egyptians and unless they bring them up to us, we rarely get any of these. What do you think?"

"He's very young to be responnsible for such a mission, but an excellent idea all the same. It would be good experience for him, but he should have a strong leader."

"I would not make him the leader, not this soon, we could leave that positiom up to the Nubian, General, Nehsi, and he could be second in charge." Then as an afterthought "You know he has the makings of a leader, already. Just an observation."

"I've noticed that too. But, the other, it.s an excellent idea."

"He can take four or five long ships with the proper number of military and oarsmen He can trade for spices, ivory, animal skins, aromatic trees, etc. It will keep him busy for several months, or longer. They should. attempt to bring back as many of the trees as possible and they should be kept wet so that survive the arduous trip back" all of this surprised Senenmut as he did realize her knowledge of such mundane things, "and he should take enough slaves, preferably the black ones, they will get along the people of Punt.

CHAPTER SIX

Tuthmose III looked at his stepmother when she explained her idea of a trade mission to the Land of Punt, suspicions aroused by her offer. He was sure that the offer, if not a command, possessed some ulterior motive maybe even dangerous. "The people from Land of Punt , although quite backward, have always been peaceful and anxious to do business as long as they were not being taken advantge of. Also the people of the Land of Punt were generally tranquil especially when facing superior forces, which they know we possess.

"Nehsi will command the expedition, and you will represent the pharaoh and our government."

"Why Nehsi, he's not even an Egyptian?"

"He is a seasoned leader, and you will have lots to learn from him. We have many important missions for you in the future, so be patient, my illustrious stepson. You have much to learn and General Nehsi will be a good instructor for you and your future."

"I think that I could handle it by myself" a note of objection in his voice "Why doesn't the pharaoh make the decision?"

"He has through me."

"I'm sorry my Queen, I would rather hear the details of the mission from him." Contempt in his voice.

"He has given me the instructions and I am giving them to you," Standing her ground.

Tuthmose turned on his heels and without a word left.

"How did it go, my lady? I sensed some objection from the tone of his voice."

"I did too, he'll follow my orders, albeit reluctanly."

"As I said before, he seethes inwardly, and bears watching." Said Senenmut, who had been within earshot during the entire exchange.

"I know.'

"What really bothers him is the ineffectiveness of your husband, the pharoah, and why he thinks he would be better and that we would all be better if the pharoah would make an unprecedent move and resign. You are making all of the decisions, but they don't have the impact as if they were coming from him, the pharoah" and carefully "and your feelings on the matter?"

"We must wait for Tuthmose to decide and if he doesn't survive, then I will be pharoah."

Two Pharoahs

It was obvious that Ma'at-ka-Ra had given the matter some thought as her husband seemed to deteriorate phsically before everyone's eyes, especially Tuthmose III.

"Yes." Replied the thoughtful Senenmut.

"I have several projects in mind that I want you to get involved in when?"

"When?"

"The time is appropriate." An ever so mild hint that she did expect Tuthmose to live much longer.

Tuthmose II was a person almost relegated to the past, and yet he still lived, and he was there, accompanied by Isis, to see Tuthmose III's expedition off to th Land of Punt. Both parents hugged him and wished for him to have a successful trip.

Hatshepsut and Senenmut, in the pharaoh's box had earlier extended good wishes and much good fortune to her stepson and watched as her husband, ill, and barely supported by Isis and as she helped him to the pallet provided for him, she looked up at Hatshepsut, a look of contempt if not loathing on her face..

CHAPTER SEVEN

The expedition to The Land of Punt incorporated five boats, each one seventy feet long with thirty rowers and seven sails per boat and a compliment of sufficient military personnel, all led by the Nubian general Nehsi. In a minor positiom was Tuthmose III a future pharoah and unhappily subordinated to the Nubian. They had been given intruction to bring back frankinsence and myrrh, the exotic trees to be kept wet so that they may replanted per Hatshepsut:orders.

Also, Hatshepsut requested that they bring back an assortment of animal skins or hides, ebony, gold, silver, electum, *antyu,* and a few live animals, preferably lions and tigers,

They departed from Quesir on the Red Sea and a contingent of well wishers from the palace were there to see them depart. The boats were assisted by giant sails made of durable cloth and made so they would withstand any inordinate winds. The boat and sails were designed by Senenmut with the suggestive assistance from Ma'at-

Two Pharoahs

ka-Ra Hatshepsut, not a pleasant thing for Tuthmose III to observe. But he would think about those things when he was on his long mission and perhaps, just perhaps he could devise a solution. But situations would evolve which would interfere with his improvised solutions.

The Egyptians, under Nehsi, landed in 'gods' land, as it was called by some of those who were enamoured with the strange land of incense and strange people. An earlier expedition had brought a small black dwarf who had entertained the Egyptian court for years until He mysteriously died. The people, unlike the Egyptians were quite dark, almost reddish-black, their hair long with, in many cases had a reddish tint and unlike their guests quite tall.Although in spite the differences in their height, a general good will existed among them.

They were met by their king, Parakin and their queen Aty, who welcomed their guest from faraway. For many, if not most, the assemblage of tall dark men, who may or may not be friendly, as they were carrying weapons, long and fashioned like spears.But for centuries there had been periodic trade missions, back and forth, between the two lands. The general friendliness was exhibited by both of two countries to each other.

Nehsi assured them their intentions were peaceful and that they were a trade mission ordered by the Pharaoh of Upper and Lower Egypt and extended the many gifts that they had brought for that purpose. A skeptical king was hesitant, but the queen Aty was less dubious about accepting the tokens of Egyptian respect.

Philip R. Clark

All of the visitors were amazed by the contenance of the queen, She was quite fat, having layers of flesh overlapping each other. She moved very slowly and the excessive flesh flopped as she moved. It was a source of amusement to the onlooking visitors, who could not restrain themselves. But the queen was unfazed by the laughter and even joined their guests in the amusement, obviously familiar with the jocularity she inspired, as grotesque an image she presented.

The group preceeded by the king and his slow moving queen who continued to be amusing to the following Egyptians and they entered the nearby village and a large single room which served as the palace and the center of the government. The houses they passed were on long stilts, some fifteen to twenty feet off the ground. Some of them were actually built over water. The houses were uniform in so far as styling, as all of them looked like beehives with circular thatched roofs. When asked about the houses and their elevations the reply was simple "Protection from marauding animals." And he took his scepter and pointed to a lion laying on the ground in the shade of one of the houses and which barely looked up as the party passed nearby.

With some assistance from a Puntite and with some communication skill the trades were completed to the agreement of each party. The Egyptians felt they got far more than they had planned. In addition to the trees which Hatshepsut had wanted, more frankincense and myrrh trees, well bundled and wet down, than they had planned, they also traded for and got gold and silver, ebony, fragrant unguents, ivory and some exotic animals, including some lions and to the point that all five boats were laden to almost the sinking point. The trip back to Egypt was uneventful in spite of the illnesses suffered by the few Puntites who wanted to migrate to Egypt.

An additional event occurred on the way back from the Land of Punt, Tuthmose III became acquainted with two of the palace guards who were assigned to the trip and who, like he. had reasoned that when Tuthmose II expires the mantle of power should go to a man not Hatshepsut, a woman. Although Tuthmose III was only fifteen at the time he still felt that he was more qualified to be Pharaoh., even at fifteen years of age.

"Are there many like you, that have the desire for a male potentate?"

"Most of if not all of the palace guard" exaggerated Neti. The most senior of the two. The speech quite guarded as they both aware of the gravity of the situation and the possible consequences, should their conversation be made public.

"And we could easily persuade the slaves we are bringing back along with the palace slaves to join us." Offered Menes.

"We must plan, and you will both be rewarded if it works out, which I am sure it will."

Little more was said between them for the balance of the year long trip.

CHAPTER EIGHT

When the expedition to the Land of Punt returned they were met with an assorment of troubling news. In fact things were not as well as all had hoped. Tuthmose II died in the arms of his minor wife, Isis The illnesses which had beset Tuthmose II most of his life finally took him. The result was that.Ma'at-ka-Ra Hatshepsut remained alone at the helm of state and preparations were being made to elevate her to the status of pharaoh..

Tuthmose III immediately challenged her, saying as a son of a deseased pharaoh, he stood in line to be the next pharaoh.

But she, clever or not , called on the gods and their representatives stating that she was the choice of the Temple of Amun and that she was the divine wife of the god Amon-Ra. And she recalled how he had appeared to her Mother when she in the womb and asserted

that she was most noble woman and that He had appeared to her by saying of Hatshepsut "*Welcome my sweet daughter. My favorite. The King of Upper and Lower Egypt, Ma'at ka re Hatshepsut, thou art the King taking possession of the two Lands"*

These divinations were more than Tuthmose III could handle and the conversation between the two ended without resolution.

When Senenmut heard of the dialogue, what was said and the outcome, he cautioned her again that Tuthmose III still seethes with jealously and possesses unbridled ambition in spite of his young age. The months long trip to the Land of Punt tended to add a certain maturity to the young aspirant. "I suggest the lady be aware of her stepson and his desire to be pharaoh". A note of caution he had delivered for quite some time. "I have told you of this since he was a mere boy. I firmly believe that his mother, Isis, is behind a lot of the agitation. The whole matter is illogical and hypocritical as far as organized government, as we know it, is concerned."

"Well spoken, I shall remain aware. He is much too young to be pharaoh. His time will come after I am gone."

"And the coronation?" He asked.

"It shall proceed as planned. The priests are tending to some of the formalities. I am making some personal changes befitting the situaution.---"

"And?"

"You know that most Egyptians expect a man as pharaoh and although I am not the first Queen, that honor goes to

Queen Sobekneferu as she was the first and few problems were encountered then."

"But. She never tried to present herself as a pharaoh----"

"So?"

"The focus has always been, with that exception, upon a male King or Pharaoh who is considered the earthly manifestation of Horus, a male god. And you would have to be succeeded by your eldest son. And you have no sons" and at that point Senenmut hesitated for a moment followed by "yet". And he arched his eyebrows in a knowing way.

"There is always Tuthmose III, who now as Tuthmose II's son would logically follow me. He is much too young now and too impulsive to be pharaoh. Seasoning is most important. Were he to become Pharaoh, I fear for Egypt. There are many peoples outside of Egypt who wish us ill."

"The Hykos could become a problem again."

"Agreed." Responded the Pharaoh-elect. "It may turn out that Tuthmose III has a future in the military, first." And with that Tuthmose III became an incidental thought, no longer worth talking about.

And then as a change of thought "Maybe you ought to get in touch with Ineni, the great architect and builder. I have several projects in mind and we should move ahead on them."

"What ? May I ask?"

Two Pharoahs

"I would like to build a memorial to Tuthmose I, my father, we've discussed it before."

"To the great Tuthmose. Do you mean the twin obelisks to be placed at the spot you personally selected and approved?"

"Besides that something spectacular, not disrespectful, but different,"

"I have had an idea that I would like for you to approve."

"I'm sure you do, but can we discuss it in a day ot two. I'm expecting some priests from the temple and I think I see them coming now on the other side of the courtyard."

"As you wish Ma'at-ka-Ra. Tomorrow will be fine. Or tonight?"

She looked at him, her eyes dreamy, and nodded assent.

"Tonight, my sweet Queen. Until then." And he looked around to see if anyone was nearby. They were alone, so he gave her a short kiss.

CHAPTER NINE

The delegation of priests from the Temple of Karnak came in to main room of the palace all bowing respectfully from the waist as they entered. They were undisturbed as they passed Senenmut who was leaving at the same time.

A spokesman for the group immediately got on message "Ma'at-ka-Ra, Hatshepsut, we like to express our sorrow at the death of your husband, Tuthmose 1I, he was a good man and undoubtedly is resting with the gods. He will be watching what we, the alive, will do when we replace him with another" being careful not use any phraseology which could be misconstrued "but after the death of the great Tuthmose II, there remains one, his son, even if by a minor wife" and he paused to catch his breath, "Tuthmose III, to be the logical heir" catching his breath again. And he bowed respecfully to be imitated by the majority of the priests present.

"Are you speaking for yourself or has my stepson been talking to you in the short time he has been back from the Land of Punt?"

Two Pharoahs

The frustated man shook his head in a circular motion, reflecting neither a positive nor negative answer.

And at that moment, she used the divine propaganda she had been saving for just this occasion.

"My lords" addressing the assemblage of priests from the temple of Karnak "Amon-Ra spoke these words as I was born *Welcome my sweet duaghter, my favorite. The Kingdom of Upper and Lower Egypt, Ma'at-ka-Ra Hatshepsut, thou art the King. Take possession of the lands'"*

Words in and of themselves were adequate to dissuade the most opposed among them. She had spoken the sacred words from Amon-Ra.

Another stepped forward and said "The gods have spoken, we will continue to make preparation for your coronation." They all bowed and backed out.

The preparations were elaborate and lengthy as many people worked to make this coronation, one for a woman Pharoah, but it wasn't without naysayers who vocally intimated that the position should be filled by a man.

And the alternative emphasis was not lost on the heir presumptive, who was doing little to change peoples' minds.

The plans for the coronation went ahead per Hatshepsut's instructions and on schedule. The throne room with the image Amon-Ra behind the throne and thereby behind Ma'at-ka-Ra Hatshepsut so when she took her place as the head of the government she did so with the approval of the gods.

At her request, Senenmut collected a quantity of black hair which she directed a servant to thread into a piece of cloth and form into a beard glueing it in place by the whites of eggs and a woven band attached on each side so the it could tied behind the *nemes* she intended to wear. She went behind a screen and spent a few minutes as she changed her attire. She put on *kilts*, covered her breast with a plain piece of white cloth, put a series of gold bracelets, placed leather sandals on her feet with leather laces going up the calf to the knee. In the waist she put Tuthmose II *Pharoah's dagger.* She reentered the room and faced Senenmut and asked him to help her don the *nemes* which was placed over her head and covered the front of her breasts. When complete she faced Senenmut and asked him to assist her in placing the *khepresh* on her head. She turned her back to Senenmut and fitted the mock beard in place, then turned around to face Senenmut again with following remarks. Expecting some remarks about her new attire.

"They want a male Pharoah and now they have one"

"Except that we both know that under all of the regalia is the woman I love' and then he suggested that she remove the mascara to complete the disguise "and where and when do you plan to be so attired?"

"Well what do you think?"

"Very impressive,"

"It's more than that, it's brilliant."

"But will it fool everybody, I doubt it. Especially your stepson.

Two Pharoahs

"I don't plan for him to be there"

"Where---?

"I'll tell you later."

Senenmut reached over and placed his hand under the *nemes* and could feel her soft breast "you're still there, no matter what, and that's all I care about."

CHAPTER TEN

'

"But I want to be there for your day, your coronation" Tuthmose replied to request made by the Queen.

"In Nubia, we are facing another revolt so I want you to go there with an ample contigent of military and search out the leaders and respond properly."

He remembered how Tuthmose I had handled such aggravations and relished the opportunity to demonstrate power as Tuthmose I had when the matter came up before. Tuthmose I had put to the sword almost a half a thousand miscreants thereby nippimg the matter at and in its origin.

Reading his mind she said "I don't want you to do what your grandfather did. Just ferret out the leaders and take care of them. In other words 'no blood bath'"

He bowed and turned away and as he was leaving she said "Assemble what ever troops you need and you can leave

Two Pharoahs

immediately, or as fast as you can." He looked back and barely nodded as he departed.

"The proper and correct thing to do" said her vizier, who was standing by and this was seconded by her companion Senenmut. "it will keep him occupied so that he cannot do anything else in his usurpation endeavors."

She was wearing her normal clothing and after the vizier left "how do you think that he will take the change in your clothing?" Asked Senenmut.

"It is my intent to be so attired at all formal functions. It has to do with the people who expect a male ruler. Which reminds me, that I want you to commission a statuary depicting me so attired to give credence to the concept so that the populace will feel confident with me pretending to be a man. You, of course you, know the difference and I hope that you accept the-the- the disguise or shall we call it a charade."

"Yes, my lady. As you wish."

And it eventually charged the minds of many Egyptians, who accepted Hatshepsut as she wanted to be.

The coronation was an elaborate affair and many of the nearby potentates were in attendance and those from afar were properly impressed as they should. If any mention was made of the Pharaoh's attire, it was done out of her presence making acceptance almost unanimous. In a historic sense Hatshepsut unusual attire became the hallmark of her recognition.

She assumed all of the titles normally accorded to a pharaoh with one main exception, she refused the title of 'the Bull' in obvious recognition of her own feminity.

The absence of Tuthmose III at the affair was noticed by those who mostly had strong feelings that *he* should be the legitimate pharaoh instead of a woman dressed up like a man to pass on the absurdity of the disguise.

The lavishness of the coronation was not lost by envious potentates from afar and this would lead to some changes which would take place in the not too distant future.

Tuthmose III, intentionally excluded from the ceremonies, was busy trying to round up enough support among the palace guard and from there to the armed forces. He was finding that he was less successful than he thought he would be. He purposely took Neti and Menes with him in the expedition to put down the revolt in Nubia., hoping that they would be of assistance. Whereas, sentiments were strongly in favor of a male pharaoh, the loyalty shown Hatshepsut was surprisingly strong.

The minor revolt to which he was dispatched turned out to be just that, a minor revolt. The leaders were quickly rounded up and dispatched to wherever they deserved. The bloodletting was kept at a minimum with only the leaders executed and the minor members were spared. For which those spared were grateful and made a point of thanking the pharaoh. Tuthmose cleverly diverted the plan for mercy to himself.taking credit for the decision.

Neti and Menes remained loyal to Tuthmose III and said that they would support him in his mission, however both felt that they would be rewarded for their loyalty, and as time went by they were rewarded with promotions and increases in benefits, all compensation for their loyalties.

CHAPTER ELEVEN

Senenmut was closeted with Ma'at-ka-Ra, she in her normal attire and they were going over a number of projects she proposed "How are things coming on the two obelisks for my father's memorial?"

"They are being carved as we speak---"

"Yes, in the quarries at Aswan?"

"I guess that, it is the only place where we could get enough limestone in one piece for two such monuments. Please make them simple, no ornamentation, but there will be nothing like them in the Valley of the Kings, or any place that I am aware of. The only problem is how to transport them. We can use huge rafts and tow them down the Nile. I have almost two hundred people working on the carvings alone. I'll probably need another two hundred to transport them and still another two hundred to assist in the erection."

Two Pharoahs

"How do you intend to anchor them down?" the question surprised him

"We will bury the bases and seal them in, they will be in two major pieces and reassembled on site."

"Where are you getting the workers?"

"Most of them are slaves, Hykos and Puntites."

"Also would you start my mortuary temple now. Something really different. Also I'd like for it to be at Deir el-Bahri up against the mountain and one for yourself nearby, so that we can be together in eternity. Don't let me see the plans. I want to be pleasantly surprised."

A dejected Senenmut, who with his architect partner, Inenei had made an elaborate mock-up of Hatshepsut's mortuary temple and wanted the time to show it to the pharaoh. She sensed his disappointment and asked him if he had something to show her, which he did, and he took her hand and led her to another room. Where he was able to show her how her mortuary temple was planned and how it would look when completed.

And to her delight he showed her the mock-up of her mortuary temple which would be by all comparisons, magnificent. It would be where she had designated. "We can call it 'Djeser-Djeseru', *'the Holiest of Holies' after the pharaoh*, very appropriate don't you think? And it will be located in Dier el-Bahri, on the west side of the Nile, in the Valley of the Kings. It will be nestled up against the mountain, as a backdrop. As you can see, though this is in miniature."

"I'm impressed. It's beautiful."

"It will consist of three terrace going up the main building, as you can see which will have a series of columns across the front which will be on both sides of the entrances. As you can also see, there will be three building and your sarcophagus will be located on a pedestal in the third building. The first two buildings will be a museum covering your reign and your accomplishmets."

"I am truly impressed. And where is yours?"

And he pointed to a smaller building adjacent to Djeser-Djeseru "Is that close enough?"

"Perfect."

The feelings between Ma'at-ka-Ra Hatshepsut and Senenmut grew even closer after the demise of Tuthmose II,. And she awarded him ninety-three separate titles during this long relationship, from tutor to lover to trusted advisor, and nothing seemed to adversely affect the relationship. She was responsible for the building of literally thousands of monuments, but the real designer and builder was Senenmut and possibly more important was his association with the famous Ineni. The two of them literally covered the country with their fine works. However Senenmut referred to her as his inspiration, a thought well placed and well rewarded.

In addition to his other many tasks, he took on the tutoring of Neferure, the supposed daughter of Tuthmose II, but he knew better.

Two Pharoahs

With Tuthmose II dead she encouraged him to be more outward in expressing his feelings toward her and told him that those moments of affection gave her great solace in her time of need, especially as she conducted affairs of state. Under his tutelege she made several official appointments and pronouncements, some of which remained for long periods of time, even beyond her reign.

Senenmut's only objection was her penchant for wearing the clothing normally reserved for men, but, in time he became accustomed even to that. When she wore the clothing normally accorded women of her stature, he could easily see the beautiful woman that he loved, trim, revealing and appealing. Just as she had been since they first moved into a more intimate mode of activity. She outwardly expressed her love for him and he reciprocated.

But what of Tuthmose III while she ruled over a peaceful and prosperous Egypt? He continued to muster allies in an attempt to usurp his stepmother, all the time seething with jealousy, sometimes to the point of distraction. He mounted several attempts to overthrow her only to have them all fail. But nothing seemed to deter him.

He did, of his own volition, make several non military incursions into Palestine and Syria investigating the possibility of future military action. Neti and Menes and a growing cadre of loyalists accompanied him.. In both cases they found that it would have been simple to acquire those lands, at least in the areas they were able to research. They appeared to possess no organized military with which to repel a possible invader.

Philip R. Clark

In a friendlier mode he approached Hatshepsut with the idea that there were open lands that ought to be brought under Egyptian rule. At first she rebuffed him, then after extended pleadings he persuaded her that it could be done with a minimum force and with little danger to the Egyptians. She agreed and during that period cleverly appointed him as co-regent extending his power mainly for military and external affairs. At the time he was still quite young, probably around nineteen or twenty years old.

He leaped at the opportunity, and even more at his appointment as co-regent giving him a modicum of power which he felt was the least that deserved in the light of logical rules of succession which would automatically give the title of Pharaoh to him.

But, her vizier and her private advisor, Senenmut, both expressed fear that to yield as much authority as she had would only lead to his grasp for more power and eventually to the position of Pharaoh. She assured them both that this would not be the case and that any authority conferred on him could easily be withdrawn.

The official appointment was made at the palace and was a grand affair attended by all of the notables at the time, even some of which had travelled some distance to be there for the occasion.. All of the priests from the temples were in attendance, the high priest representing Ra, made the official announcement with Hatshepsut's approval and acknowlegement that Tuthmose III was to be the co-regent over both Kingdoms of Egypt and those

Two Pharoahs

lands which are supplicant, as of now and into the future.. The garb, properly accorded to some of such high station, was donned by the newly appointed co-regent and he properly paid homage to the pharaoh, who smiled in acceptance. He looked stunning and the pharaoh attired in her male costume tapped him lightly on the shoulder affirming her honest approval. The idea of the pharaoh and her co-regent standing side by side accepting the good wishes from those in attendance was a sight for all to behold.

Unfortunately, the apparent amity between the two was more one sided than it appeared, Tuthmose was, for himself, thought this the whole matter was a ploy to anneal harsh feelings which has long existed between his stepmother and himself in his own mind and he carefully concealed those ill feelings for the present. An extraordinary feat for him.

CHAPTER TWELVE

No one, especially Hatshepsut, expected the degree of success the Tuthmose III had as he began the first of what would be seventeen campaigns as he moved to annex part of Palestine. A number of cities fell easily under his relentless attacks. His troops plundered relentlessly and without mercy. He returned bearing huge amounts of tribute and gifts with special ones for Hatshepsut, as the ruler. Additionally many slaves were acquired, some with special talents and skills in farming, husbandry and domestic proficiencies.

When questioned by Hatshepsut about the his conquest, Tuthmose was reluctant to give any details, "Were there lots of deaths?" She asked.

"Which side?" almost impolite.

"Both sides?"

"We lost a few. We, also, killed a lot of their men, those we that we could, and those who would not surrender,

Two Pharoahs

some of those we brought back as slaves, which you know about. We captured several small cities which were not protected very well, so the task was relatively simple."

"The women?"

"We brought a few of them along with us and we left the rest behind to help in the repopulation. In most cases individual men were in charge of the cities and they have a small council of men, elders, all of which survived. We left them all there to manage the affairs of government, subject to Egyptian rule and they know full well that they are now under Egyptian rule and control. We also left a cadre of Egyptians, officers and soldiers, to maintain order."

"And the women?" She asked again

"You know what happens in situations like that?"

"Yes, but that doesn't.make it any better."

"A Pharaoh should not be concerned about such mundane matters." Was the sarcastic reply and Tuthmose III turned on his heels, back to her and left.

Hatshepsut considered recalling him, but then thought better of it.

Senenmut, who as usual, was standing within earshot, looked at the departing man, then turned to Hatshepsut, "That was right no matter how impolite he was, Ma'at-ka-Ra. It doesn't make any difference how much he dislikes it, he must answer to the Pharaoh, and with proper decorum. And I wouldn't have called him back

Philip R. Clark

in this instance. You will have other confrontations and my advice to you is that you use your pharaoh's position to let him know who is the Pharaoh. And as an aside, I'm not sure, as your advisor, that I would have made him co-regent, at least until he was a little older and little more mature. But in spite of that, you have to admit he did well."

"However, no matter how we look at it, he has some rightful claim and if he lives longer than I, he will be the pharoah. In spite of the problems we have incurred , I respect him and all of his pomposity. I only wish that the relationship was better."

And it did improve, as Hatshepsut had Tuthmose III marry her daughter, Neferure even though she was only twelve years old, two years under the normal minimum age of fourteen years. It helped insofar as the union was concerned as Neferure had come to worship the young Tuthmose III, even though there was an estrangement between her mother and her now son-in-law. An important aside was that it assured the Tuthmose dynasty, if and when they had a child particularily since it was believed by all that Neferure was the daughter of Hatshepsut and Tuthmose II, and none dared doubt it. The temple priests blessed the union and contemplating on the pair surmised that there should adequate heirs to carry on. They knew full well that their very existence depended on it.

And as far as the dynasty was concerned, it did work out well as within a year Neferure was pregnant surprising the pharaoh and the parents-to-be.

Two Pharoahs

In spite of the happy occasion the feeling of amity between the pharaoh, Hatshepsut and Tuthmose III it did not last. He did not feel that being co-regent satisfied him. He was more determined than ever to unseat the sitting pharaoh and take over what he devised was rightfully his. All of that, in spite of his newer relationship with the pharaoh brought on by the his marriage to her daughter. It was not long until the sense of animosity returned.

And Hatshepsut, fully aware of this, however dismaying as it was, planned another campaign for the young co-regent.

CHAPTER THIRTEEN

"I know that you have planned, or shall we say considered, further expansion of Egypt to the east, what exactly do you have in mind?" asked Hatshepsut of her now son-in-law as well as step-son.

Not one to hesitate "There are great lands to the east of Egypt and also to the north across the Great Sea."

"What makes you think it so?"

"Our sailors and our sea traders have seen lands over on the other side."

"Have they seen people?"

"Yes and we have traded with some of them. Nothing of value by our standards, but that does not rule out their potential."

"Alright," with some hesitation, "you have my permission."

Two Pharoahs

"Permission for what, my lady?" Miffed at her outward reluctance, and showing it "I'll take General Neti with me."

"General? That's a long way up from palace guard."

"He's a good man and he deserved it. He served us well on our Nubia expedition."

"Loyal?"

"Very"

"I thought so." And Tuthmose did not catch the inuendo.

"Assemble whatever manpower you think you will need and requisition the necessary supplies for your campaign. I will be praying to the gods for your success and safety, my son-in-law." And she advanced to embrace him, only to have him turn away before she reached him.

Senenmut and her vizier were present at the time and both noticed the rebuff. She, now dressed in her normal linen gown, well coiffed with her normal hairpiece, the odor of the perfumed oils emanating from her body as she had applied an extra potion just before the meeting, all in hopes of having her son-in-law see her as a woman, rather than a pharaoh. Seeing Senenmut and the vizier standing there as possible witnesses became a possible deterrent, thus disinclined to show any signs of reciprosity at the moment. Slighty abashed, she quickly dismissed the vizier and took Senenmut's hand and led him into her private chamber.

Later as they laid nude, one against the other, he said "I'm sorry Ma'at-ka-Ra, he is headstrong, a problem of youth, he may change, but I would not count on it. He envies your position and it may never change until he is able to mount the pharaoh's throne and exercise all the power it encompasses. So be wary at all times. I approve of your using him in the way you are, he has the presence of the military and should be well placed there."

And Tuthmose again amassed an even larger contingent than he had before. The lure for his enlistees was the great potential for wealth in both booty and slaves that would accrue to them as Egypt's superior forces met the expected inferior and unprepared opposition.

Tuthmose III seemed, again to be in his element as he and the two generals that he had appointed, Neti and Menes, built a powerful army and a fleet in preparation to sail out of Egypt's northern shore to the area on the eastern shore of the Great Sea. He was sure that there would bounty aplenty to satisify the conscripts and volunteers that comprised his large army. The expected treasures, considered to be extravagant by comparison to his previous campaign. And as it turned out such was the case.

Tuthmose III was only twenty-one years of age when he commanded a force of 10,000 Egyptians against an equal force of 10,000 defenders of the plains in front of Megiddo. In spite of the advice from his military advisors with his selection of the plan that his forces advance through the mountains passes, adjacent to Mount Carmel, instead of going to long way around either north or south sides of the mountains the element of surprise compketely stuprfied the enemy as his forces then overwhelmed the unsuspecting Canaanite defenders takng possession of the area and two cities along the way. He then laid siege to Megiddo for eight months until the city surrendered, A major victory for the young would-be pharaoh.

He returned to Egypt, victorious, having captured three cities, including the important Megiddo, coming back with an amazing quantity of treasure in gold, slaves and animals. Hatshepsut expressed her appreciation and congratulations for a job well done and gave him an special award, a monument of his likeness and commissioned by her and designed by Senemut and placed in conspicious place where it could be seen by those who have an interest in the project. Tuthmose was pleased with the attention, but emotionally did not waver in his opinion as to who should be the pharaoh. Being a co-regent did not satisfy him. And no matter how well things appeared, he was not dissuaded.

"In summation, I would like to report that in addition to the capture of all of Canaan we have opened the way to proceed north to Syria and east in to areas that seem to bounded by two great rivers which flow south, not like the Nile. There appears to be arable land much as the Nile valley is after the rainy season. Some consideration should be given to the idea that we consider advancing further east into the lands beyond '

So fierce were his campaigns that Tuthmose was able to extract 'tribute' from those countries who fell under the Egyptian sphere of influence.

CHAPTER FOURTEEN

But the truce with Hatshepsut was short lived. The air between them cooled and she found herself wearing the male clothing more frequently to allay fears of her performing the duties of the Pharaoh, more as a Pharaoh than as a woman..

The relationship proved to be evanescent in spite of the good will extended by the Pharaoh. to Tuthmose. His successes in his brief campaign had garnered new found loyalty over a broad spectrun of the population, particularily among the young and the military.

The temple priests also began to waver. This was most evident of all in the Temple of Atum, where the priests were a formidable force to be reckoned with. The country's vizier came from the Temple of Atum, a fact which in and of itself helped to create the tension that existed.

Senenmut remained Hatshepsut's primary advisor as well as her lover. In those moments of intensity, she was always sure of his help and devotion and the tender moments

Two Pharoahs

they had in her bed. He assured her that her throne was not in peril and that the enthuasism for Tuthmore was only temporary. But all the same she asked him to create a monument depicting her in her full male regalia, beard and all and that he take some liberties with her body design and that she appear with larger muscles.

"That is going to be difficult, my lady. I see you as you are, small and dainty.But I will try."

"Use your imagination."

"Do you want to have your breast to be obvious?"

"I am not ashamed of them. Should I be?"

"No, my love, you shouldn't"

"As a matter of fact, why don"t you do two of them in different poses and we'll put them in different locations."

"But you will not be able to fool your subjects wih such a disguise."

"Some may be influenced by what they percieve, and in the end I will be the winner."

"You know best, Ma'at-ka-Ra. As you would expect, I acquiesce to you wishes. Do you want those images of you to have full headdress?"

"Yes, both, the *nemes* and then the *khepresh*.over the other It's what the people expect of their pharaoh",with a lot on emphasis on the last word and the feeling of determination by her was not lost on Senenmut.

"Also, while we are on it how are doing on Mortuay Temple at Deir el-Bahri?"

"The plans are almost finished. The first drafts should be ready for your approval any day now. It will be beatiful and quite different with terraces and columns across the front. I think that the pharaoh will like it."

"Do you plan to plant some of the myrrh trees in the terraces as we originally planned?"

"Yes, but we may have to go back to the Land of Punt. I don't think that those that we have now will stand the transplanting. I would like to have fresh trees thereby assuring that they will survive."

"That's another reason to send another trade mission down there, and which will give both of us another reason to send Tuthmose down there."

"Well said my lady."

CHAPTER FIFTEEN

The idea did not set well with Tuthmose. He resented making another trade trip even if he commanded it, which he did not on the prior trip. "There will be a minimal number of military to be taken on the trip as no campaign of a military nature is planned nor authorized. Just enough military to assure your protection.' And added "We need some more myrrh trees for my Memorial Mortuary Temple, those that we have will not stand transplanting. And while we are at it you may as well bring back more ivory, ebony and gold. Senenmut will give you a list of what we want on this trip as well as the list of trade items they will probably desire" It was an order from the person to his mind, the usurping pharaoh and a woman at that, and he resented it and made it evident.

"Do you want these myrrh trees to be large?"

"They will grow, if they are treated with care and kept wet in transit." Her knowledgable

Philip R. Clark

reply.

"How does a *pharaoh* happen to know so much about such mundane things?

"That's why I am pharaoh."

Tuthmose looked at Senenmut "I'm learning too. I'll have those lists for you by day's end " Offered Senenmut, trying to calm the waters.

Saying no more, Tuthmose abruptly took his leave and met with his two primary allies, Neti and Menes, "Like or not we are goimg back to the Land of Punt for some more trees to decorate one of Ma'at-ka-Ra's projects designed by none other than Senenmut, who else."

"Are we to go as a military campaign?" Asked Neti.

"Obviously not, unless you call uprooting trees a military feat."

"You are becoming cynical, not becoming of your youth."

Tuthmose said in response "It is a poor way to use what military we will be taking with us. The Puntites are a peaceful people and it would easy to turn the Land of Punt into another series of Egyptian nomes. But that is in the future."

"It seems as if you may have some plans along that line for in the future." Said Nemes seeming somewhat excited by the prospects.

Two Pharoahs

"I have lots of plans for the future, but they will have to wait, for now, at least"

"Why? Aren't you the co-regent with *her*?" Menes replied

"It takes time." a short pause to allow that to sink in "And planning"

"Planning?" Said Neti.

Tuthmose looked at both of his friends for a long time, then "You know that when she dies, I will become pharaoh, so it is just a matter of time."

They both shook their heads as if to expect the obvious.

"She's quite concerned about her future, or why is it that she is planning to fill the country with   monuments to herself? Have you seen any of them? They are everyplace, and a lot of them in her male costume, which is rediculous"

They had seen them and agreed, carefully agreed. In spite of the situation they still had to be careful about what they said and did. Nothing else was said for the moment.

"We need to plan the trip to the Land of Punt" and he left the two trusted generals to retrieve the lists from Senenmut.

"Our friend seems a bit impatient, doesn't he?" Said Menes

"Yes. He feels he belongs on the Paraoh's Chair, not Hatshepsut. Do you agree?"

Philip R. Clark

"As a soldier, I think Tuthmose has some valid ideas. There is no reason why we make trips to the Land of Punt, or wherever, when there is so much more to be had by expanding to the north and east and make Egypt into a great power, maybe the greatest power on earth."

"We had better watch our tongues, all the same."

"Indeed."

"Have you talked to any of your people?"

"About those thing we discussed on our last trip to the Land of Punt?"

"A few of those I most trust."

"And you?"

"Much the same. We really have to be careful. One man, Akhohop, a corps leader is really a man who is loyal to Senenmut, and therefore the pharaoh. He drowned when we were loading the trees in the Land of Punt."

"Accident?"

"It wound up looking like it. So there are forces who do not agree with our point of view."

And the two generals parted both musing about their futures and the future of Egypt.

CHAPTER SIXTEEN

Senenmut approached Hatshepsut, a troubled look on his face, and asked for a private session with the pharaoh, "I have some troubling news to convey to you, my lady." The chamber was cleared and she asked "What could be so serious or important that my vizier could not be privy to the information, when there's little in matters of state that I do not share with him?"

"Not even he, my lady. should hear this." And he looked about to be absolutely positive before he would continue. "My lady, as you must know that we both have enemies in places even in the government that are determined to do you harm."

"Places, where?" thinking that it was strictly a figment of his imagination.

"In the military for one. I have my " and he chose to word carefully "my allies who have the interest of the pharaoh in their devoted hearts. I have purposely placed them in places and positions where they might overhear or become aware of any matter we might consider treasonous."

Impatiently "Please tell me what you are talking about."

"A trusted person, one that I would trust with my life, was killed as they loading trees on the boats in the Land of Punt."

"An unfortunate accident? "

"Probably not. You see he and one other overheard associates talk about how they would like to depose and replace you with Tuthmose III."

"I am sorry that someone loyal to me is by the nature of it in mortal danger. But that doesn't surprise me, a lot of people would prefer a man as their pharaoh. That's the main reason I've resorted to the male costume in most formal occasions."

"I'm sorry Ma'at-ka-Ra, this is more serious than some feeble desires to have a male pharaoh. The man, Akhohop, a man you have met" she nodded in assent "he was pushed and fell into the water, then the tree was rolled over him to hold him down. When a man, a Puntite, a slave, I think, tried to assist him, the slave was told to back off and given a lash at the time. My confidant saw it all and told me."

"I'm sorry for Akhohop, but why does that give you the idea that there is a plot ?"

"Akhohop has been one of my most loyal friends, reliable. He is the one who gave the early warning that I passed

Two Pharoahs

on to you. He picked it up from some soldiers, just in everyday conversation, then according to the other person just before the accident he and Amentohop overheard two of the officers discussing the matter of your future with Tuthmose"

"Now that is interesting. Are you sure?"

"Positive."

"Any suggestion?"

"I think you are and have been a good ruler. Fair, Egypt's doing well under you. Far better than your husband and better than the two of you together. Tuthmose desires for Egypt is to expand our boundaries north and east and he is bothered that you do not agree with him."

"That's the difference between us. I'm for peace and friendly relations with our neighbors. And as long as I am pharaoh we will pursue this course. Tuthmose may have grander ideas but he'll have to wait his turn and time."

"As you wish, but please remain alert. For both our sakes."

He stood on one foot then another looking at Hatshepsut and thinking how beautiful she was and if anything happened to her how devastated he would be.

She watched him intently, almost reading his mind "Don't worry, I'll be alright. Tuthmose may have ideas about taking over but it will be over my dead body."

Philip R. Clark

He thought about what she had said, then reached for her hand to comfort her, she smilrd and said "I had more than one reason to ask for privacy."

And Senenmut began to help Ma'at-ka-Ra remove her male pharonic costume.

CHAPTER SEVENTEEN

The trip to the Land of Punt proved to be more successfull than the prior one. Tuthmose with a smaller campaign body of personnel and fewer boats returned to Egypt with a larger number of the valued myrrh trees and twice the quanty of gold and electrum, much valued by the Egyptians,.than they had before. All of this was to the delight and surprise of Hatsepsut. They had also brought back some Puntites as slaves who probably thought that their life would be better in Egypt than the Land of Punt.

Hatsheput took the occasion to invite Tuthmose to a celebration for his success in his recent trip. He felt that this was an unusual gesture intended to gain his loyalty in his backing of the Pharaoh, particulrily in her mission to build a number of new structures. Tuthmose was grateful and accepted the acclimations with adquate grace. His only negative comment was that he performed better than the Nubian, Nehsi. She attempted to mend the existing acrimony that prevailed between the two of them. And it seemed to work, as he, excluding the one remark regarding Nehsi, seemed quite happy with conditions of the moment..But it was not long before he broached a subject of interest to him.

"I still think that the future of Egypt lies to the north and beyond." He explained. "those people exist and at this time do not represent a problem to us. But in time they will all join forces and we will become the objects of their aggression."And Hatshepsut recalled to herself the words of caution that had been conveyed to her by Senenmut a short time before and then said "I seriously doubt that there are any people or civilizations that will be ble to match our power and our military. We have the largest number of troops on earth today, capable of handling any enemy."

"Admitted. But what makes you think that there are no potential enemies out there someplace?'

Hatshepsut could only shake her head. "It's just a feeling that I have"

"But you or we do not know what may exist beyond those borders as we know them. Our advance troops report that they have seen people, light skinned, large in size much like some of the Hykos people that were here in the past."

"Were they as organized or advanced as we are?"

"I think not , but we have not entered their cities, at this point, so there is no way we can assess their potential at this time."

Two Pharoahs

"We'll discuss this later." A way to dismiss the young man. "Incidentally, I heard that one of our valuable officers was killed in an accident, I suppose, loading the trees on your excursion to the Land of Punt?"

"Yes, Akhohop was a good man, and it was an unfortunate accident. Completely unavoidable" was his quick return. Not easily deterred "Yes that would be good, if we could discuss some of our options later. I look forward to the opportunity. and quite important to Egypt" whereupon he politely took his leave and no more was heard of the matter at that celebration in his honor.

CHAPTER EIGHTEEN

"Do you mean that she seemed not to have an interest in going beyond our borders into other lands?" asked Menes when told of the conversation that Tuthmose had with the Pharaoh.

"I have a better idea. We, as Egyptians, must secure our lands and the way we do that is to take over those immediately adjacent lands creating a safe area for all Egytptians. I don't think she realizes how vulnerable we are. We spend a lot of our treasure erecting monument to all of the gods and past leaders, when we should be building on our military."

"Yes, but when?"

"When? What?"

"Do you plan to depose the pharaoh?" Menes had just broached a forbidden subject and Tuthmose winced and lowered his voice approporately

"Sooner than you think." Was his muted reply.

Carefully, "what do you have in mind?"

"I have a few ideas, but no definite plans. I'll keep you apprized of my plans as they develop."

"Whatever. Remember I am with you, no matter." Said Nemes.

"I am counting on you and a number of others who seem to be of like mind."

"Others?"

"Yes, there are several people who have commited, quite a few."

"Do you think that *she* knows?"

"I'm not too sure, but I'm not going to worry about it" a pause "yet."

"As an aside, you also have to be concerned about Senemut. He has the pharaoah's ear and he has allies in the military."

"He has more than her ear, he sleeps in her bed with her and has since she was about fourteen. My wife, Neferure, is one of their offsprings."

"But I thought she was the daughter of Tuthmose II and Hatshepsut?"

"Not possible, they never occupied the same bed."

"You mean Tuthmose and Hatshepsut?"

"Yes, she loathed him, and I might add he did not care for her either. She was the older domineering sister. So Senenmut, being appointed her tutor took full advantage of the situation and you see what happened. My father, Tuthmose II knew of the situation, but he could care less, afterall he later had his Isis, my mother, to keep him busy. And from what I've heard she kept him very busy."

CHAPTER NINETEEN

Tuthmose III received a messenge from Hatshepsut, who wanted to see him immediately, which turned out to be a great surprise especially in the light of their late conversations. "Another trade mission to Punt, I imagine. Probably need some more trees" he told his young wife, Neferure, who immediately moved to defend her mother.

"Mother has greater things in mind for you, you just have to be patient."

He immediately left following the special messenger until the reached Hatshepsut's quarters.

She, accompanied by Senenmut, her vizier, a group of priests from the temple and the Nubian general, Nehsi. The sight of the latter was somewhat disturbing, but the Pharaoh was exhibiting great amiability asking questions about the health of her daughter, whom she had seen earlier in the day along with her newborn grandchild

Philip R. Clark

Tuthmose was disarmed be the amiability, and especially when his mother-in-law came up to embrace him.

 "I would like to discusss with you some of your ideas regaring a possible venture beyond our acknowledged borders.'

Immediately alert and doubting the sincerity of the inquiry, Tuthmose began to detail some of his ideas telling her how he felt that to ignore the problem would only invite measures, possibly to the extreme, from other peoples, as they add sophistication to their inferior civilizations.

"And you think that there are civilizations out there" waving her arms in a circular fashion, "that are capable of waging a successful was against Egypt, defeating us, subjugating our people?"

"Need I remind the pharaoh about the Hyksos?"

"They brought some good, and we learned from them, before expelling them."

"What else besides disruption?"

"The chariot, horses, lots of things."

Their ideas of a single God and their idea that all of us came from a pair in some far fetched place. We were much better off to be rid of them." Said Tuthmose, somewhat testily.

"But not all of them, in spite of that man called Moses. We have kept a few of them as our better slaves, and those that were freed or earned their freedom have turned into good Egyptians." And added as if to defend an active and prosperous minority. "Those that remained have pretty well assimilated into the Egyptian population. And we are able to adjust without any real problems. But, my son, what specifcally do you have in mind?"

She's serious he thought "We have succeeded in Canaan and there are areas and peoples to the north and east of that. We have captured a few city areas, like Megiddo, which is now part of Egypt and we have placed respnsible people and military to administer it.. The people there are much like the Hyksos. They are for the most part a light skinned people and in some cases their eyes are light too, and they, some of them have yellow, red or white hair. I imagine that if we ventured farther we may find a lot more."

"How do you know this?"

"We get lots of information from people we come in contact with. Also the traders who use the Great Sea, tell us of other lands and peoples all over.'

"Are they as advanced as we are? Do you think?"

"It's quite possible.".

"More advanced?"

"It's quite possible." He repeated.

A frown crossed the fair pharaoh's face, unusual for her since her public demeanor always seems sunny. Thoughtfully. she turned to her vizier and her Chancelor, Senenmut, and asked "how do you feel about this?"

"I think his point is valid.and deserves consideration." Said Senenmut and the vizier agreed.

"Well, what does my son-in-law recommend at this point?"

Apparenly taken back by the pharaoh;s possible reversal, "We should prepare ourselves for another possible attack similar to the one that we suffered under the Hyksos. We should take the iniative and attack our potential enemies before they attack us."

"Who are these 'potential enemies' you speak of with such certainty?"

"I feel there are organized armies, which unless we stop them in advance, may see some advantge in trying to conquer Egypt. I have heard and we have on good information that there are countries, maybe as powerful as we are, and we do not need to be on the defense in the event of an attack."

"These countries, where are they?"

"Across the Great Sea, to the north and to the east. We have seen their traders, some of which have visited our ports."

'What do they look like?" Immediately curious.

"A lot like us only their skins are almost white, they have different colored hair, at least that's what I've been told and I told you this before. Also there are peoples far up the Nile, beyond the high mountains, they are black, much like the people from the Land of Punt, but they're far from organized. More like small tribes or families."

"You seem to know a lot." An honest statement.

"I've always tried to keep an objective eye on the future."

"What do you have in mind, should we entertain some form of action?"

"I would move troops, not large quantities of them, but small groups to reconnoiter, surreptitiously move outward from Megiddo and report back any groups of people massed into a cohesive units that may be Egypt's potential enemies of the future. If there is one Megiddio, there just may be more."

"Amass a plan on what you would do and how many men, boats and what supplies that you may need for an effective campaign and the time that you will need to accomplish your goals."

An amazed Tuthmose backed off bowing to the pharaoh "Three days , my lady" and departed, smiling and nodding to Senenmut and the vizier."

The vizier, who had listened to the entire interchage between the pharaoh and Tuthmose finally made a statement "I hope that the headstrong young man doesn't take us into a war after so many peaceful years under my lady and her father." Completely disregarding her husband. Tuthmose II.

"He won't, I will not let him get out of hand."

CHAPTER TWENTY

On the other hand, Senenmut looked at the situaton and concluded that this was the perfect way to rid the Pharaoh of a tirng nuisance and it was his idea to have Tuthmose III kept busy chasing his dreams of an Egyptian Empire.

"I think it is a perfect solution, at least for the time being. There is no limit to his ambition and that does not bode well for you, my lady."

"You don't think that he would do something, well something---?" and she was having trouble actually verbalizing what she was trying to say.

Senenmut eased the situation "Do something to you, personally, it's possible. The idea that to have made him co-regent may only feed his ambition."

"That was your idea."

"I know, I know, and it may have been a bad decision. Sending, or shall we say *letting him* go and lead this campaign without interference will give us time to prepare for the next situation."

"He is our daughter's husband and they seem quite good together and you know how close she has been to us , especially you."

"And Tuthmose spends more time with one of his harem wives."

"They've been married for a little over five years now, and he's been able acquire harem wives so soon?"

"Yes, I thought you knew."

"I do now. Any chikdren?"

"No, but one of them is pregnant."

"Any of them of royal blood?"

"I don't think so, ask Neferure, she'll know."

"She's so young, only eighteen years now." Meditatively., "and already a mother."

'Going back to Tuthmose, I have gotten good intelligence that there is a conspiracy fostered by Tuthmose to overthrow you, either peacefully or forcibly. That is the reason I encouraged you to give him more power by allowing him to lead a campaign. It will take time and if he is successful so much the better for Egypt, and I think he will be successful and you may want to give him something, voluntarily of couse, to ameliorate the situation. Still another way to look at it, if he is victorious Egypt and you will look better."

Philip R. Clark

"I can tell you something Senenmut, my love, I will not step down, no matter what or how well he does. He will have his time after I die and I hope that's a long time off.'

"And as I do, also." And he moved toward her and started to dismantle her male garb until she was almost nude with only a flimsy full length gown after he had removed the kilt and headgear. "You are as beautiful as you were when first we slept together maybe more so now that you are a full grown woman. If anything happens to you, I'll die." Then added "now that we've found something to keep him occupied for a while." She reached him and placed a passionate kiss on his lips.

"Isn't there something else we can do?" as she led him to her private chamber.

"I'll think of something."

CHAPTER TWENTY ONE

Tuthmose wasted no time in preparing for the planned campaign. He easily assembled a force twice as large as the previous one. The success of the prior one and how it had enriched the participants was widespread and a magnet for many like minded recruits. The training preparatory to the campaign was severe and as a result the troops were hardened and prepared to fight and ready to expect the worst should it come.

Three times as many chariots and a equal number of horses were assembled. The charioteers were worked so that the training ground on which they practiced was reduced into a maze of dust as group after group would feint charges toward each other.

The pharaoh paid a visit to the troops and congratulated Tuthmose III and his two generals Neti and Menes for the expertise demonstrated by their troops, albeit it was difficult to see anything, the dust was so thick.

Additional troops were busy preparing the boats, over two hundred of them. Boats that will be carried manually overland a short distance to the Nile. And thence loaded with the carriers, equipment, food and water and the ground troops floated and rowed down the river to the Great Sea. The sails are then unfurled and a destination of north and east was set, the troops ready to meet any enemy wherever or whoever they might be. Tuthmose, flanked by his two loyal generals, Menes and Neti, all were looking eagerly forward to what may lie ahead.

The charioteers with their chariots and horses would advance on the east side of the Nile where they would be met at Tanis, at the mouth of the Nile, by the boats filled with the men and supplies. A two day rest was in order, time to assemble. Then they advanced and surpised the Canaanites by seizing two more of their cities. They plundered both of them, killimg at will or rounding up those healthy enough or young enough to be returned with them to Egypt as slaves, irrespective of age or sex.

The bounty was not as great as the prior one as the area was more destitute and the pickings were less than expected. The largest single item of bounty was the slaves. They were a mixed lot with most of them being light skinned and the men were mostly bearded, unusual for the traditional smoother faces of the Egyptians. The decision to take almost as many females as males assured them that in some cases families remained intact.

A period of rest ensued as the slaves were sent back to Egypt, guarded by troops from the Egyptian forces. Other troops were sent north to probe the possibilities of future movement into the area. These were met with

Two Pharoahs

fierce resistance from a well armed group of soldiers and found out that they were another race of people called Syrians who were bivouacked a short distance from the advance point held by the Egyptians.

The fighting that ensued, as a result of the surprise meeting, left many Egyptians killed and a few were captured and taken prisoner. The rest seeing that they were greatly outnumbered fled back to the join their group and reported their encounter with a masssive army. The report ascertained that even though the contact, although brief, was violent enough to convince the forward group of Egytpians that their respective forces were seriously outnumbered and possibly could be defeated should the two bodies meet each other. For the Syrians, who until now were basically unaware that the Egyptians were advancing into their area. They, both armies, abjured further contact for the present. The Syrians were in the area to make contact with the Mitanni and were taken aback by meeting another force, and one which would offer considerable armed resistance.

Tuthmose III, in his contentious contact with the Syrians, although minimal in size, realized that there was a sophisticated civilization on Canaan's northern border, one that possibly could significantly challenge his concept of Egyptian superiority in the immediate area. Normally a person with great bravado, he in this case, decided to wait for another day. He gathered his troops and the booty and returned to Egypt.

Nevertheless, he returned to Egypt to a heroic homecoming. The pharaoh was pleased with the outcome as well as the larder. He immediately approached her to authorize the next campaign, this time to Syria. "I'm convinced that the Syrians' intentions are not honorable. They,too, seem to have expansionistic inclinations, and they may just have us in mind."

The Pharaoh immediately took exception to Tuthmose's idea "It has been my plan and my desire that *we* rule over a peaceful and posperous country" with an unusual emphasis placed on the '*we*' which the alert Tuthmose picked up immediately.

"*We* need to be able defend ourselves against any encroachment by a possible enemy."

"Have you seen one?"

"Maybe."

"Where?" asked the persistent Pharaoh.

"Just above Canaan, I think." A not very convincing reply.

"How do you really know?"

A ltttle indignant by the questioning "We saw a group of men, bearded, large men, and we successfully engaged them." Not the entire truth, since he had lost a number of his soldiers and a number had been taken as prisoners while no Syrians had been taken prisoner.

"Saw?"

"A contingent had been sent out to explore the area north of Canaan and report back. They unfortunately came upon a small army of these people which we assumed

Two Pharoahs

were Syrians" then the truth " they, our men, were mostly slaughtered and a few of them made it back to our lines and reported back to me that there was a large body of men, an army, at that location. General Neti was in charge and he was able to escape and rejoin us and made the report that I am giving you."

"Syrians? How do you know that?"

"We have had some commercial contact with them before. A mostly backward people."

"And they have big marauding army close to Canaan?"

"Yes."

"What about our interests in Canaan?" a now interested pharaoh asked.

"I do not know what the disposition of them will be. Without some additional military attention, they are very vulnerable."

"What do you suggest we should do?"

"We should reinforce our garrison in each location so that they will be able to defend themselves, and- and we should build our army up and repeat our excursion into that area and fight the Syrians forcing them back to wherever they came from."

A deep frown crossed the Pharaoh's pretty face as she looked to her vizier, then to Senenmut and watched as they both shook their heads in disapproval. "We'll discuss it later, You have done well, Tuthmose, surprisingly well. I have commissioned a number of memorial monuments which will be placed in obvious positions of honor" She then turned away from Tuthmose and nodded to her vizier and Senenmut to follow her, leaving Tuthmose and his entourage in a state of mystifcation.

CHAPTER TWENTY TWO

Tuthmose did not take the obvious snub gracefully, as a matter of fact, he was incensed., infuriated. He took solace with his two newly appointed generals.Neti and Menes. "She is wrong. Her idea of a peaceful and prosperous Egypt, puts Egypt in a very tenuous position, no matter what she thinks" He picked up a stool and crashed it into one the pillars to show his displeasure with the pharaoh.

"It seems like our plan has reached a point of possible fruition?" said Neti as he stood nearby.

"No not yet." Responded Tuthmose "but the time is rapidly approaching, out of protection for all of Egypt."

"What have you planned?" asked Neti.

"Only to replace *her*, and soon."

"How soon?"

"Soon enough." And her looked at his friend a little closer. "Do I dare trust him?" he thought in spite of the fact that he and Menes have been quite close. But with something so delicate as deposing our leader. If either one of them turned on me I'd be dead in a flash. Best I keep my plans to myself for the time being. They were both palace guards until I took them out, however they still have connections among the guard.

"How soon?" Neti repeated.

"Soon enough?" disturbed by Neti's insistence.

Neti feeling that he had gotten all of the information he could at this point, changed the subject "Is it true that the pharaoh has commissioned a monument and a stele of our last campaign to be placed in your father's, the great Tuthmose II, tomb?"

Even Tuthmose III knew that his father had been a poor ruler, and that was the main reason why Hatshepsut was able to wrest the power from him while he consorted with his mother, one of his harem wives. But why the flattery from such a minor person. His suspicions were again aroused. "Yes, I've been told."

"She must have thought more of our expedition than we thought she would?"

"Why do you say that?"

"Well it was pretty well known in palace circles that it was really a plan to get you out and away from the palace."

"And who told you that?"

Two Pharoahs

"'Akhom, he is one of Senenmut's helpers and he is related to one of my wives. He was drinking and he let it slip out."

"You heard it?"

"Yes, from my wife, Djeserit, who, like her name, is holy and wouldn't lie to me."

"Senemut has entirely too much influence on the Pharaoh and that's a weakness she has." His mind working at breakneck speed "can you get Akhom to talk to me?"

"I think so, but what should I tell him was the reason?"

"You'll think of something." And dismissed the general as if he were an underling, which in reality he was.

Akhom was impressed by the attention he was getting from one of the most highly placed persons in the government. Neti approached the young man and told him how important Akhom was being as close to Senenmut as he was. "I have been thinking that what Djeserit told me about your great talents with stone and how well you work with your superior."

"Senenmut has been a great teacher and I admire him and his wisdom. I enjoy being in his presence and being a trusted associate."

"You have done well, Akhom. Have you ever considered the military. If you did as well there you would soon be a very rich man." A tack used by Neti to influence or at least entice him with wealth which he did not have being a close associate to Senenmut. "Are you paid well?"

"Well enough. I am happy."

"I need an assistant and you came to mind, so think about it and let me know if you are interested. You would get a share of the spoils."

"Any danger, fighting, you know?"

"You would be like a historian. No fighting. There are to be great events, battles against formidable enemies and you will only be recording the events as they happen."

"I'll talk to my wife about it and Senenmut---"

"I wouldn't talk to Senenmut" he interrupted. "Which wife?"

"Harere. I only have one and that's enough."

"Children?"

"Two, a boy and a girl."

CHAPTER TWENTY THREE

Senenmut took his lover aside and told her of the events of the last few days "Akhom, you've met him, he is one of my best scribes, a good man. He has been approached by general Neti to join the military as a historian where he can record first hand events as they happen."

"There are not going to be any further military 'events' as long as I am pharaoh."

"I know that, Ma'at-ka-Ra, as I know your plans, to which I concur, but, and a big but, I have told you that there is a nascent desire to replace you as pharaoh, primarily led by Tuthmose and an assortment of people including Menes and Neti, former palace guards."

"Yes?"

"Well, I believe that he is reliable and loyal, especially to you, my lady, consequently he could be an important asset for us were he inserted into their inner sanctum."

"How would he convince Tuthmose and those around him that his intentions are sincere?"

"It wouldn't be easy, but possible."

"I am definitely interested in keeping an eye on Tuthmose. The foreign campaigns, although successful did little to keep him sufficiently occupied and lower his early expectations, as a matter of fact just the opposite has occurred. No blame for this" as Senenmut had fostered the idea of foreign campaigns, "it was inevitable."

"Akhom is intelligent enough and with a little coaching by me, he will be a good person to have in the right place at the right time."

"Would it be enough to infiltrate their group and not arouse suspicions and at the same time and become privy to their inside information?"

"Yes, I believe that he could do the job. If you agree, I'll talk to him" and he added "secretely, of course. And I suggest that you have no conversations with him about it, my lady"

Akhom expressed interest in the plan as it was laid out by Senenmut "There shouldn't be anything dangerous about it. It would be a case of your getting their confidence so that they will be unafraid to discuss their plans in front of you or directly to you. To add to the credibility for your displeasure with me and the pharaoh, we will discharge you, only temporarily, but that can be your *cause celebre* for your unhappiness with the pharaoh and me."

Two Pharoahs

"I'd advise you wait a few days after you are discharged, as a matter of fact let them contact you." Said Senemut.

"I wouldn't do anything untoward to you or the pharaoh." Replied Akhom.

"We understand that and we are counting on you to carry out this very important mission."

"But, in time Tuthmose will be the pharaoh and I will be responsible to him as will you" was his studied reply.

"True, but I seriously doubt that Tuthmose will use me, even spare me my life, and the same applies to those who are close to the pharaoh, Hatshepsut which includes, I might say is you and people like you. It's dangerous, yes, but calculate the options and the alternatives. Need I say more."

Akhom was convinced and considered the thought that he would be able to play both sides if he had to. In the interim he'd participate in the idea.

Akhom, suddenly discharged with but a flimsy excuse, his speaking with general Neti about leaving the service of Senenmut, was chided for his disloyalty and discharged forthwith. He went home, unhappiness evident.

"What's the matter Akhom?" asked Harere, his wife, as he arrived earlier than usual and was obviously dejected.

He explained that he was discharged for having contact with general Neti, a contact which he did not initiate, but one that he admitted he had "Afterall, he is related to you."

"And they discharged you for that? You have always been close to Senenmut, helping him every way that you can. And for so long? What are we going to do? You needed that job, we did."

"I am going to contact Neti and take him up on that offer the be a military scribe for the army. He seemed eager to use my particular talents."

Akhom was busy clearing out his work area, first the cleaning of his tools and then placing them in a wheelbarrow that he used to transport them as needed. He was looking duly unhappy for a man, who has spent all of his working life and as an assistant to his idol, only to be summarily dischaged for something so insignificant as talking to Neti, an associate of Tuthmose.

However, General Neti was pleased that Akhom had changed his mind and welcomed him into the military, immediately giving the task to create a stele on the battle they had with the Canaanites on the plains outside of Megiddo. He wanted it to be large and include, obviously, flattering representations of the activities of Tuthmose and himself.

CHAPTER TWENTY-FOUR

"Did you get things worked it out?" Asked Hatshepsut.

Momentarily befuddled by the question "What is that, my lady?"

"Your arrangement with what's his name: Akhom?"

"I'm sorry, my lady, I've had my mind on something else Yes, I think we have someone in place whch should reap us great benefits within a short time."

"What do you think we should do if something really develops?"

"Treason? Probably."

"I don't think that would be possible. He's too popular after his victories in the campaigns."

"Possibly so, but what else could you call it ?"

"If only he could wait his turn, would be nice and appropriatate. But I think we should play this along and if anything truly egregious comes up, I will confront him on the matter."

"I wish you well, Ma'at-ka-Ra, I wish you well."

On the other hand Neti was meeting with Menes and Tuthmose and telling them of his apparent coup by bringing in a very disgruntled Akhom. "what was the reason for him to so easily switch loyalties?" asked Tuthmose, more than a little suspicious.

'Senenmut, himself forced the issue by discharging him out of hand, no excuse nor rational reason for doing so." Answered Neti.

"Exactly, and there may be another reason that we are overlooking. What if he was *given* to us for nefarious reasons. We should be very careful around him until we can improve our feelings about him. In the interim, we should be extremely cautious about what we say in his presence, extremely careful." Said Tuthmose. "We need something to test his loyalty."

"We'll think of something."

And they did by simply concocting a story through the military that there was a slave uprising in Aswan which would put a stop to the many monuments that Hatshepsut had commissioned Senenmut to complete. Since there was no way to easily verify this it seemed the ideal plot, given the distance from Memphis and Aswan

Within days the information was surreptiously conveyed to Akhom by way of ordinary conversations in his presence. True enough the information was relayed to

Two Pharoahs

Senenmut and Hatshepsut. Wisely Senenmut, who knew well enough that if such an event actually happened it would have a paralyzing effect on their elaborate building program, dismissed the rumor for what it actually was, a rumor. And one which tended to test Akhom's continued loyalty to the pharaoh.

"What makes you think that what we have heard is a rumor?"

"I have no definite information to counter their claims, but I think it is a test, to see if such informatiom is leaked back to us and to see how we respond. Hence we do nothing,"

"What if it is true?" asked the pharaoh.

"That is the chance we should be willing to take." Replied the advisor.

CHAPTER TWENTY-FIVE

As time passed Neti and Menes became closer to the former palace scribe, particularily a former palace employee, and a highly disgruntled one at that. And on his part he was the perfect ploy. He carefully sifted through any information he was able to get and ascertain that which is important enough to convey to Senenmut.

Within a short period of time, he was able to determine that the conspiracy was reasonably wide spread and that there were several members in quasi high places privy to the information and in agreement with Tuthmose III. Some rationalized that the country should have a male ruler and the heir apparent was ideal for the job. Some even fostered violence to reach this determination, but they were a small, albeit vocal group.

Senenmut received the information as it came and as Akhom was passing the data along and certain preventative measures were taken, many people were assigned to different jobs and many in different locations, all of which tended to weaken the coalition.

Two Pharoahs

This did not go unnoticed by Tuthmose, who just refused to believe that all of these acts were merely coincidence. A year had passed since Akhom had joined him and his organization. His work had been exemplary as well as his demeanor and loyalty. At Neti's recommedation, Akhom had been allowed into the inner sanctum of the private conversations which covered the private discussions about an array of items including items intended to depose the sitting pharaoh.

Tuthmose called Menes in and asked him if he had any idea how so much private information seemed to get into the pharaoh's hand and which result in actions which are hindering any progress they were making. "I do not know what you are talking about." Replied Menes aghast at the peculiar questioning.

"I think that we have an informer in our midst. A lot of plans are being usurped before we can actually move on them. How do you feel about General Neti?"

"You should be sure that Neti is loyal to you. He would give up his life for you."

Properly or improperly nettled by the pharaoh's insistance on taking his more talented men out of the military and using them to advance her many construction projects"The pharaoh has diverted many of our key associates to her mortuary temple she is having Senenmut build on the Nile at the Peak of Thebes. I went down there to see why she was draining as many people as she could. It is spectacular, larger than anything built to date. It is terraced at three levels, as far as I can see, over one hunded columns across the front. There is supposed to have over one hundred images of *her and her father* placed all over the project and a sarcophagus for her father and one for herself. I believe that the project is intended to disturb our plans for her replacement."

Burdened down with a series of complaints, Tuthmose approached the pharaoh and was disarmed by her obvious desire to make their meeting nonconfrontational and to ease the negative hubris from their relationship "I've really needed to talk to you. As the co-regent, which you are, your advice is important to me at this time in particular ---"

"As much as Senenmut?"

Taken back, but not showing it "I do value Senenmut's opinion and advice, as I have for many years, now, he is very wise, but he does not know everything."

"For example?"

"I am curious about those possible encroachments you seem to fear."

"I hope that I am not repeating myself, but I do fear countries and peoples that we have had but minimal contact with. There are civilizations and people out there who just may have intentions that are contrary to ours and us. And I say this in all candor, we have come to believe that our potential enemies are not like those in the Land of Punt or the Hyksos or the Canaanites, when in reality beyond those lands may be a people or peoples who wish us ill and just may be waiting for that moment when we are most vulnerable."

Two Pharoahs

"Which means that we are at that moment in our history?"

"I think so, my lady."

"What makes you think that, we are sufficiently powerful to repel any unwelcome intruders?"

"But are we? Your massive building program, intended to provide much needed work for our people, but this is done at the expense of the military. Some of my key military people are engaged in your projects. I have been down to see your mortuary temple and it is magnificent beyond belief, set as it is, at the head of a valley overshadowed by "The Lover of Silence", Peak of Thebes where you as a goddess, and those before you preside over the necropolis. It will be beautiful when completed. But so many men and slaves are being diverted from their regular tasks to complete it and all of the other monuments you have ordered."

"And you believe that the utilization of manpower has weakened the military?"

"Yes, we are far under our minimum optimum strength. Our forces have been decimated."

"O, Tuthmose, you as co-regent and in charge of the military affairs of the Upper and Lower Kingdoms should have warned me of the potential peril so that we would have been more prepared in the event of some unwarranted attack."

"I have, my lady, have you forgotten?"

Which she definitely hadn't. "I just thought it wasn't too big a problem."

But in reality it had been fully her intention to keep Tuthmose and his cadre of loyalists so occupied that they would have little time to conspire with each other. She had made sure that Neti and Menes were on separate projects some distance from each other and from Tuthmose. But common sense now came to the fore and she decided to give the future Pharaoh some tasks for which he was more than qualified.

"Please take the time to lay out just what your plans are to secure our country."

He did not believe his ears. "I have given them to you some time ago."

"I guess that I may have forgotten them. Would you please?"

Intent as he was that her forgetfullness was intentional "Yes, my lady, I'll have them ready in five days."

"A smart move. That will keep him occupied" Said Senenmut when told of the way Hatshepsut's dialog with Tuthmose had gone.

"In all fairness, he just may have a point" said Hatshepsut in response.

CHAPTER TWENTY-SIX

And three days later, Tuthmose was seeking an audience with the pharaoh.

"You are sooner than expected. I hope that you have not forgotten anything in your haste.

"I have been thinking about it for years."

"Years?"

"Yes, since the last campaign, when we talked about the possibilities and you demurred, saying that Egypt was not looking to increase its territory."

"In reality, I still do not see or envision anything currently dangerous, but I can be convinced if your argument has credibility. A small change in my attitude, I might add."

Tuthmose thought he was talking to another person instead of the heretofore stubborn Hatshepsut. It momentarily softened his attitude toward her and he hastened to explain his plans.

"Well, my lady, beyond the areas we have already acquired, east toward the high mountains lies a momentous piece of land which I believe to be occupied by a superior civilization, not equal to us, but almost and I think that they are acquiring lands and people as fast as they can, I do not know exactly how many there are. What I do feel is that they are destined to become our enemies one day and to deter them would be to reach them and defeat their forces before it becomes inevitable that they reach our sacred land.

"Also, I feel that with our superior forces and weaponry we will be able to defeat them, all the while subjugating them, or bending them to our will, In other words strike them and defeat them before they try to do the same to us."

"You have thought this out well, my son" using a familiarity which he resented.

"For years."

"As you already know, I think that peace is far preferable to war. But as pharaoh I must look at all sides of the issue. Lives are at stake and we should tread lightly in matters such as those. I personally don't feel that we are imperiled. I see nothing beyond our borders that is menacing to the point where we should engage them." And Tuthmose's heart sank, "however I could be wrong and your experieces in Canaan and at Megiddo tend to solidify your argument," again he could not believe his ears.

"How large an army would it take, could you guess?"

"Twenty to thirty thousand."

"Get back to me as soon as you can with your grand plan on how this, that you speak of, can be done." An elated Tuthmose could not believe what he was hearing.

"I'll call a council of my leaders and be back to you within four days." And he abruptly went up and kissed her hand, the first physical contact he had with her since he couldn't remember when. Nor could she.

There was not a whole lot that Tuthmose and his council had to do. He had been planning for quite some time as a matter of fact he was prepared at the end of the last campaign. With his council they figured that the minimun manpower they would need would be thirty thousand combat ready troops and another ten thousand support men.

The soldiers, excluding the charioteers would be armed with swords, spears, maces, cudgels and daggers. The charioteers will be armed with long spears and bows and arrows. The bows will be the flexible bows, as developed by the Hykos and superior to the more rigid ones used before that. Each bowsman, including charioteers will be equipped with twelve copper tipped arrows. For the chariots, ten thousand horses will be needed, an almost impossible task, but one that would be accomplished.

"And how long will it take you to build up your supplies and manpower?" asked the pharaoh.

"Including training, about one handred and eighty days" He replied. And she looked toward Senenmut and her vizier who both nodded their approval.

Philip R. Clark

CHAPTER TWENTY SEVEN

What no one had considered was the involvement of Isis in the grand conspiracy to remove Hatshepsut. Afterall she was the mother of a future pharaoh and she hoped to see it in her lifetime. She had broken off from the other 'harem' wives and with the baby Tuthmose III had moved into palatial dwellings befitting the mother of a future pharaoh. Tuthmose III remained with his mother and excepting those times he spent with tutors and trainers. Mother and son were quite close and she coddled him preparing for what she believed was the inevitable.

As he grew and entered the military, she was never but a short distance away. And during his lifetime Tuthmose II tried to get close to his son, but was disuaded by Hatshepsut. And as he was losing the clasp of power to his royal wife , and older sister, his familial relationship with Isis, his 'harem' wife became even stronger.

As Tuthmose III began to accumulate friends and allies in the military and they visited. Isis, still quite young, and almost as beautiful as Hatshepsut, turned the eye of one

Philip R. Clark

of her son's military aides, Menes, now a high ranking officer in the military. Seeing his interest, she was flattered and began to use her feminine charms and was met with more than a casual interest.

"Are you married, Menes?"

And was rewarded with "No, my lady, it is difficult to be married and in the military at the same time. I prefer the military if given the choice and fortunately I have."

"Is that a permanent answer, meaning do you plan to remain in the military?"

"As long as your son will keep me," then added "wherever he goes, there go I."

"And if he becomes pharaoh?"

"When he does, I will be there, I promise, if he will have me,"

Catching on to the 'when' she said "such loyalty needs to be rewarded."

"I serve Tuthmose, I used to be a palace guard and he took me out of that environment away from the pharaoh and her sycophant, Senenmut and he has rewarded me a hundred fold."

"And you have no wife? Have you ever?"

"Oh, I have had women, but no wife."

"What kind of women?"

"All kinds, Canaanites, Puntites and Hyksos."

Two Pharoahs

"No Egyptian?"

"No, not yet." And he seemed embarrassed by her inquisitiveness.

"You should." and she moved a little closer to him, her perfumes filling the air, the aromatic odor was almost too much for him as he moved away.

"Your odors are entrancing," he commented, as he held his nose up and breathed deeply.

"Do you like it?" Still holding her distance.

"Yes. Wonderful."

She sensing that she may be overplaying her hand, left his side and went over to the nearby couch and bade him to sit with her.

He looked at her and for the first time noticed how alluring she was, her flimsey gown revealing a still youthful body and he was immediately aroused by the sight of her and was happy to see Tuthmose III who at that moment appeared.

He looked knowingly at his mother and pardoned himself for the untimely intrusion.

"Not a problem" and Isis rose and went to her son's side, kissing him lightly on his cheek.

"There are things I must attend to, so if ---" she clasped Menes's hand for what he believed was a longer time than he had expected, her body exuding the aromas that he had never been subjected to before.

Philip R. Clark

"We must talk again, Menes' and like a vapor she disappeared.

"Yes, you must," came from a smiling Tuthmose.

And this relationship was enhanced by Menes's more frequent visits to the Tuthmose palace, something noticed with great interest by Tuthmose, himself.

"Mother, Menes is not coming to see me, he can do that anytime, he is coming to see you"

Isis blushed lightly the color coming through her light tan skin, smiled, and began adjusting her hair and her outer attire,

"How old were you when I was born?"

"Fourteen. I was your father's favorite wife."

"Including Hatshepsut?"

"Especially including Hatshepsut. They did not like each other. They never occupied the same bed."

"Then how?"

"Senenmut. Your wife even looks like him. Taller than most. Grey eyes. I was the only person that your father would have anything to do with. Who was with him when he died? Your mother. Who was with him when you went on your first campaign? Me. Where was the queen? With her Senenmut. As busy as he is with all of the construction, he's never far from *her.*"

"You should be careful with your speech, things get out."

"Yes, my *pharaoh.*"

CHAPTER TWENTY-EIGHT

The following week general Menes did come to Tuthmose's mansion with other intentions. As a matter of fact Tuthmose had been called to the palace to discuss further campaigns with the pharaoh. A change from the cool attitude she had exhibited heretofore.

Instead of being attired in his military kilts, he was wearing a casual outer garment that reached the floor. Isis was not surprised to see him as a matter of fact she was planning on it, as she had taken her son's words literally. Since the conversation she had with him, she had made a point of being properly clothed and with ample applications of those aromas which he had found so facinating

She was still young, just over thirty years old, and he was about the same age and with no formal attachments. But for all of that she needed to play her hand right .

She looked him, while he stammered to say something meaningful and seeing his timidity went over to embrace him in a friendly way "I'm so happy to see you and you look so handsome not dressed in your usual military attire."

"Uniforms are not for all occasions" and she signaled for hm to sit on one of the stools as she took her place on one of the couches, nearby and he complied "And your son, Tuthmose III?"

"The pharaoh has called him to discuss your next campaign."

"They don't always agree, the pharaoh and Tuthmose."

"I know."

"He means the world to me, the gods were good to me, and to Neti, to take us two palace guards, and raise us up to command ranks. This would never have happened if I'd have remained as a palace guard. Both Neti and I owe Tuthmose a lot."

"Didn't you like your job in the palace?"

"It was alright. A lot of politics, which we don't have in the military."

"Politics?" she asked timidly.

"You have to be careful what you say and about whom."

She urged him to come over to her couch and sit beside her "One of the guards was heard saying unfavorable about the chancellor---"

"You mean Senenmut?"

"Yes" and he made a motion with his finger from one ear to the other.

She shuddered, moving closer to him "What happened, I mean why?"

"They don't allow much information out, but they called it 'treason'."

"Beheaded him?"

"Yes."

She shuddered again and moved closer to Menes and began runnning her finger through his long unruly hair "you need somebody to tend to your hair, it needs tending.you have numerous tangles you failed to get rid of earlier."

"That comes from not having a wife."

"Mistress?"

"No wife , no mistress" and he began to feel a little anxiety, afterall the woman next to him was the wife of a former pharaoh and the mother of a future pharaoh.

Isis sensed the uncomfortable condition she had placed the person next to her from all of the attention he was getting and she ceased adjusting his hair, but she did not move from the close proximity to the embarrassed man. He moved inches away only to have her move with him. She then began to adjust the folds in his outer garment.

Tormented by the close proximity, Menes asked "Are you expecting Tuthmose any time soon?'

Two Pharoahs

"Not until tomorrow."

"Servants?"

"All dismissed until the morning." How much more must she do to entice this man into some response? She thought. The closeness and the perfumed air did the trick, Soon the almost reluctant woman was on her back and Menes grappled to remove the clothes that separated them. They both were victorious. But for different reasons.

CHAPTER TWENTY-NINE

Menes's visits to theTuthmose.'s palace beacame more frequent and Isis would always in near proximity of the man. This did not go unnoticed by Tuthmose when he bluntly asked "Are you sharing your bed with Menes?"

And then a less than embarrassed woman answered, "I don't see this as your affair. "

"It is my affair, I,as a future pharaoh, don't want anything to mitigate my authority, especially your relationship with a common soldier."

"Hardly a common soldier, a general, besides you seemed to want me to pay Menes some special attention, so what are you complaining about?"

"Nothing, I guess. I just wanted you to have some male companionship, you've been all alone since Tuthmose II got sick and finally died,"

"When Tuthmose, your father, picked me as his secondary wife, I'm fimiliar with the needs of men, gave him my all.

Two Pharoahs

I have avoided all other male contact since then. I truly loved him and I hope I'm not appearing disloyal to him or his image. To be married to a god, your father, was one thing, but Menes is a man. I'm still young" and Tuthmose looked at his mother and concluded that she both young and beautiful, "so,my lord, grant me this freedom.

He looked her over noticing all of her voluptousness, probably for the first time "Will he be moving here or will you move?"

"Too soon to decide this."

"Just be careful" a caution which both of them understood.

And Isis immediately went to work assuring that her beloved moved from the cramped quarters, in which he lived to the more sumptuous mansion inhabited by her son, Tuthmose III, and her. Her plans were moving ahead, but caution was imperative.

When Menes was approached about the matter, he first feigned reluctance, but after a word of approval from her young son, relented and he soon became a member of the household.

Menes with Isis' encouuragement began to assist Tuthmose in all ways possible and in effect became his executive assistant exercising second in command power over the military.

The move was not discouraged by either Hatshepsut or Senenmut and suddenly he found himself privy to the most important military operations.

And since Neti had been resposible for the inclusion of Akhom, the former and now apparently disgruntled assistant to Senenmut, he selected him to be his special assistant. And this allowed him to be aware of many issues concerning the pharaoh. He had overheard many open criticisms of her and her policies, but nothing he could report as treasonous.Everything that he overheard had more to do with military complaints, most of which would be considered quite normal. So there was nothing to report to Senenmut.

Isis and Menes were as active as young people generally are and suddenly Isis found herself pregnant. It alarmed neither her son nor the pharaoh. As a matter of fact Hatshepsut suggested the the duo be married and that the celebration would be held in the palace and the high priests from the temple would officiate. Within six months Isis and Menes were parents of a boy whom they named Khasekhem, the same name as Menes's father, and after a pharaoh in the second dynasty. The earlier Khasekhem had been a fierce soldier, as Menes appraised himself.

Hatshepsut, truly interested, asked the proud parents to come to the palace and present their son to her. Isis refused to go, complaining illness, and Menes had to make the appearance with the baby Khasekhem alone.

When Menes and the baby returned from the palace, with him was his long time friend and cousin, Neti as their fathers were brothers.. As a threesome, they were quite close, having grown up in Tuthmose' palace together. As a maater of fact Neti coveted Isis early only to have her selected as a Tuthmose II 'harem' wife and move her to

Two Pharoahs

the main palace when she was fourteen. His lust for her dimished when he took wives of his own, but now she was married to his favorite cousin and he wasn't unhappy about how everything had happened, but he still bore a modicum of envy when it came to Isis. He was pleased to see how happy she was being married to Menes.

He frequently pitied Isis as she took charge of the ailing pharaoh when he reached death. Hatshepsut had garnered most of the power by then and made most of the decisions. This nettled Isis, who even though she had mothered a future pharaoh, remained relagated to a minor role. She had been moved to another palace with Tuthmose III, as ordered by Hatshepsut, removing her son from tutelege normally accorded to a future leader.

Isis was glad to see the entourage as they returned and was surprised that it included Neti, whom she had not seen for some time.. The baby was hungry so Isis sat on a nearby couch and nursed the famished youngster. When finished she passed the baby off to an attendant and the father.

"How did *she* feel about Khasekhem?" Isis asked her old friend Neti.

Noting the irreverence in her query, Neti tried to take the edge off the conversation "She thought he looked a lot like Tuthmose II."

She did not take that as a compliment as Tuthmose II never had a day in his life where he looked like he felt well. "*She would say that*" her voice tinged with sarcasm.

"You don't like the pharaoh, do you?"

An emphatic "*No I hate her. I would put a dagger in her selfish heart, if I had a chance.*"

Menes, just reentering the room overheard her, and chided "You shouldn't talk that way, you may be overheard."

"I don't care, I;m sure she knows how I feel."

Neti was surprised at the level of vehemence expressed by the woman.

CHAPTER THIRTY

And the day finally came when Hatshepsut called Tuthmose to the palace to discuss his plans for Syria. Heretofore she had expressed doubts as to the feasibility of the project and now suddenly seeming to be allowing Tuthmose free reign in the selection of the targets and the enemies. She did suggest Syria, however, and he concurred.

"Your plans are pretty complete and we are in agreement. Do you have an effective date?"

"Days away, just days away." And the answer seemed adaquate to her. She had made several trips to the training area and was honestly impressed with the progress and was quick to tell Tuthmose and his wife Nefeure.of her pleasure.

Whereas, in conversations with his commanders he had said 'If we are successful, which I'm sure we will be, it will be looked upon as the *pharaoh's idea* and most of the credit will accrue to *her, whereas,* the whole idea is mine and I should get credit for it." It was a picayunish expression for a man, though he was young and probably momentarily thoughtless, as he addressed the military leaders beneath him.

But the expression was seized upon by many of those present, especially Neti, Menes and of course Akhom, who was there in his duties as the official scribe.

"Maybe she will be gone as pharaoh by the time we get back" came a voice of one of those present.

"Yeah, yeah" coming from others.

"Perhaps she will be gone before we even leave."

"Yeah, yeah." Louder this time

"Hail to Tuthmose, the Pharaoh, long live Tuthmose. Long live the Pharaoh."

Akhom did not believe his ears. This was treason. However he carefully mimicked his cohorts so that there would be no suspicion as to his loyalty. Neti was particularily interested in Akhom's responses. What he saw satisfied him.

When the meeting ended, Tuthmose called on his two favorite generals, Neti and Menes and the Nubian Nehsi for a special meeting to plan strategies. All of the others were dismissed and sent to their other duties.

Akhom, now quite concerned, wondered how he would get the word that a revolt was brewing and maybe almost ready to occur. He must get the word back to Senenmut as soon as he could, but if he valued his life he would

Two Pharoahs

have to be disceet about it. He rarely went to the palace since his 'purported' problem with Senenmut.

And the opportunity did happen in the most unusual way, At dusk he was walking home, a long troublesome day behind him, and he most casually ran into his former mentor, Senenmut, also taking a walk. They passed each without even a nod of recognition and then after a few feet separated them Akhom looked back and coincidentally so did Senenmut as he arrived at a curve in the walk. Akhom went to a nearby myrrh tree, so valued by Hatshepsut, and with a sharp tool scratched the soft bark of the tree.

Since no further arrangement had been made to signal the need for communication, Senenmut waited until Akhom was out of sight and he returned to the tree and looked at the slash that Akhom had administered moments before. To damage such a tree in like manner was unlawful and Senenmut knew Akhom to be law abiding above all else. Unfortuantely, both Neti and Menes observed the unusual behavior of both Senenmut and Akhom.

CHAPTER THIRTY-ONE

Harere waited patiently for her husband at nightfall and when he did not arrive and after a reasonable length of time she addressed her mother who lived with Akhom and her since her father had lost his life on the plains of Canaan. After a lengthy wait she went to the palace and sought out Senenmet who told her, in major confidence, that her husband was involved in a subrosa task to root out any treason toward the pharaoh. Additionally, he had spoken to him earlier in the evening and thought that he was going straight home. "He must been further delayed along the way."

"But, where?"

"This is a big city, he could be anyplace, Harere." Trying to comfort her and still not show any unusual concern.

"But you saw him as he was on his way home?"

"I saw him as we passed in the early nightfall, he was going one way and I, another."

Two Pharoahs

"But you said that you had a conversation with him?"

"I did, I did indeed."

"Was it about the treason thing?"

Oh well, he thought, I've a mess of things to this point, I might as well tell her the whole story "We'd pass frequently and merely nod and pass along, this time he made a point of using a sharp instrument to remove some of the soft bark on one of the myrrh trees, forbidden by Hatshepsut, so I returned on the path where we met again and he disclosed to me certain, shall we say conumdrums which require immediate attention. He did a good job, I only hope it's not too late."

"But where could he have gone?"

"I'm sure he will be home soon. Just go there and wait. He'll show up. May have had an errand to do first." This did not satisfy the poor wife who now knew the extent, though not fully, of his involvement. She wished that he had confided in her so that she would now understand, and even , maybe, deterred him.

And Akhom was never seen again. His simple act of trying to communicate with Senenmet spelled his doom as Neti, always somewhat suspicious of Akhom was nearby amid the myrrh trees as he conveyed the information to Senenmut. He caught up with the poor man and plunged a sword into his heart and had some soldiers drag his body and cast it into the Nile.

Philip R. Clark

The die for Tuthmose III had finally been cast. There was no turning back now. The call now was for action, no more conversation. Long live Tuthmose III.

Now what?

Neti and Menes met with high ranking co-conspiritors and they collectively decided that the time for action had arrived. They could no longer talk about it, the pharaoh needed to be deposed, forceably if necessary.

Should they bring Tuthmose into their plans? No. As all realized that his reign would be besmirched if he were to assist in any overt act.

Senenmut, now aware, of a pending plot against the pharaoh advised her of their plight. "You may avoid any bloodshed if you step down and relinquish the throne to Tuthmose" an idea that she dismissed out of hand.

"I am the Pharaoh, and I will remain Pharaoh until I die" was her quick response.

'It may come sooner than you think' Senenmut said to himself "We need to increase the guard."

"How loyal do you think they are? They may all turn against us."

"I'm sure that a lot of the men are with us." Said Senenmut

"But which ones?"

"We will be careful and I will be watchful. I will have my sword nearby. Tomorrow we will get those men we feel

Two Pharoahs

sure we can trust and station them in all places throughout the palace. That way we will be secure from any possible intruders. Then you can face Tuthmose and have him call his dogs off. He will be pharaoh soon enough. So we will sleep tight tonight and I will be your guard."

CHAPTER THIRTY-TWO

A group of selected men led by Neti stealthily moved toward the pharaoh"s quarters quickly dispatching the guards that had been selected by Senenmut. The guard detail had been doubled as a special precaution, however the men selected by Neti were or had been part of the palace detail and were familiar with the palace and the habits of the occupants. The key for them was stealth. All of them removed their sandals and any jewelry or metal they would be wearing. They were to carry a single weapon each, long daggers. They blackened their bodies with charcoal so that they could be unseen as they lurked in the shadows. Where they suspected there were two or more additional numbers were assigned. All strong advocates of Tuthmose as pharaoh and extremely loyal to him. The hour selected was two hours after midnight.

They quickly and silently killed eleven guards and two staff members and the group went to the pharaoh's private chamber. As expected the pharaoh and Senenmut were in the same bed, their backs to each other. One man

Two Pharoahs

moved into position and quickly plunged his long dagger into Senenmut's heart. The man gasped and the noise stirred the pharaoh and she fell across her lover and Neti stepped forward and plunged his dagger into her chest fatally wounding her.

"O Horus" the single vocal noise emitted by the dying woman, calling out to the main Egyptian god.

PART TWO

CHAPTER THIRTY-THREE

Neti, accompanied by a small contingent including Menes went to Tuthmose's III palace and located the young man who was in bed with his wife, Neferure. They both were startled and surprised. "Awake, awake O Pharaoh Tuthmose III. The Great Tuthmose III. Long may he live and long may he rule Egypt."

"What, what are you talking about?" asked the startled and sleepy Tuthmose.

"The pharaoh is dead." Came the excited voice, "The pharaoh is dead."

He immediately asked his wife, Neferure, the daughter of Hapshepsut, to leave until he could get the details.

"Senemut is dead too."

"How? Where?"

"At the palace. They're both dead. Killed. Stabbed through the heart, both of them."

Somewhat angry now "Who did this? Who would do this?"

"I did, my lord, I did it. Egypt should never have a woman pharaoh. Now in, Egypt, we have a man as pharaoh as it should be." Said Neti unapologetically.

A shocked Tuthmose sunk to one knee and brought his hand up to his head, saying nothing. He then rose and said "I must go to my wife now, I must explain this to her now." And he left a mystified cadre of his followers.

In the meantime the noise from the crowds in the streets grew louder and louder Tuthmose III advocates, having heard the news, began a wave of destrucion throughout Memphis and as the news travelled to the hinterlands as almost all images, steles and memorials dedicated to Hatshepsut were damaged or destroyed. Days later Tuthmose ordered an end to the wanton destruction of those things that were dedicated to her in her life.

In the first meeting of his staff, a day after the tragic event Tuthmose confronted his old friend, Neti and inquired of him the certainty of his admission for the fatal act commited upon Hatshepsut by him, and he received "Yes, I did and gladly so, O Tuthmose" whereupon Tuthmose asked the the man be seized, bound and put into a guarded cell until further instructions would be given.

"Why, O why is this happening to me?"

"You killed a pharaoh, a woman, no less a pharaoh, who is the embodiment of god"

Two Pharoahs

"But, but---" and Tuthmose turned away and one could see a tear in his eye.

Three soldiers grabbed Neti just as he tried to move and forced him to the floor lashing his arms to his side. Menes broke through the crowd and moved to help his friend only to be held back by the soldiers present. As he fought his way, Tuthmose looked back and warned him that the same fate would befall him if he didn't desist "If you, too are involved, you too will also receive the punishment that will be meted out to Neti."

"I agree with Neti and in what he did, as do you. I have heard you say it."

"Never, Never did I subscribe to murdering a pharaoh, any pharaoh." Tuthmose said "take him away." Pointing to Neti.

He turned and left to go across the large courtyard that was positioned between the two main palaces. The well terraced area was ringed with Hatshepsut's myrrh trees that she so treasured and as Tuthmose went from one place to another he felt a sense of remorse "this is not at all what I planned. My hope was to bring her down in a quiet mutually acceptable way so that I could become pharaoh. No violence, just a peaceful change over was my plan."

As he entered the palace he noticed that there was a large assembly of people many of them crying or wiping their eyes. They parted to allow him through so that he could go bach to her private chamber.

Philip R. Clark

When he entered he could see the undisturbed murder scene. Blood was omnipresent, the pervasive sight disturbed Tuthmose as the scene remained as it was at the outset. The pharaoh's mostly nude body rested over Senemut's as she apparently and vainly tried to protect him. A large dagger protuded from her back, a stream of blood going down her bare back into a pool which had accumulated on the floor beside her bed.

It was an emotional time for Tuthmose. Never in his life had he felt so sad, even at the death of his father. They, he and Hatshepsut, had had their moments, but the competition was tranquil and his intentions were entirely peaceful.. He went over and touched the now cooling body and turned to the attendants telling them to remove both bodies and prepare them for mummification. "She was my stepmother. She was great pharaoh. She kept Egypt prosperous and at peace. Together, with Senenmut, they had built more monuments to our departed than any one heretofore and repaired or restored more objects dedicated to our antiquities than any one else. She was a great pharaoh." These pronouncements were very public for all within earshot to hear and if anyone would look tears were streaming down his face. A beaten foe, but a noble one at the same time.

CHAPTER THIRTY-FOUR

The transition from Hatsheput to Tuthmose III was relatively simple as she had left an orderly government for him to take over. He kept the same vizier and main staff that she had . The only changes he made were in the military, excepting Neti which he replaced with the Nubian, Nehri. The same Nehri, whom he objected to, at the outset of his campaign to the Land of Punt.

He issued an order to halt the wanton desecration of all monuments, stelae and anything else memorializing his predecessor and the deeds performed by her. However the order did not get out soon enough to stop many of his loyalists and those who were never comfortable with a female pharaoh. So, much damage occurred before the desist order was in place.

A proper period of mourning, a full moon, or twenty-eight days was declared

CHAPTER THIRTY-FIVE

Menes thought of another way to save his friend, Isis, Tuthmose's mother just might be the saviour. He would ask her to interceed in behalf of his long time friend and still a friend, he hoped, of the future pharaoh. In a minor way, he too had been involved in the slayings. All the same, he did not think that he would tell her of that specific detail. The allusion would already be there, and that was enough.

He did not want to lose his life over the matter, now that his life was reaching the best it had ever been. His relationship with Isis was paramount. He had never felt better about his life as he did now. May be, just maybe, he should be careful about what he says. "I think that the pharaoh will be merciful when it comes to the idea of punishing Neti. That's right, he will use the occasion to show a merciful side"

Since Tuthmose had moved to the main palace, his mother Isis remained in the minor palace across the wide courtyard. She was happy to have it this way as it gave her

Two Pharoahs

all the freedom she desired. She, Menes and Khasekhem could function as a family. But there was a problem, and one that Menes hoped she could resolve. His best friend and cousin was in dire peril because he led a cadre of revolutionaries in the overthrow of pharaoh Hatshepsut. He even bragged about being the final assailant. He needed to discuss it with her and soon. He didn't know which path Tuthmose III would follow. He definitely was more angry than he had ever seen him,

Sensing that he would eventually talk to her about the dilemma, she waited for him to broach the subject. Having been alerted in advance and surreptitiously about the situation she had the answer ready. "I do not think I can help you in the Neti matter."

"Think? Have you talked to your son?"

"The future pharaoh. What do you think he should do? Set a precedent for all pharaohs?"

"Specifically. I'm talking about our friemd Neti-----?"

"I know, I know, I will talk to Tuthmose, but---? I will talk to Tuthmose, my love. I do not want anything to happen to him, but I'm afraid that the die has been cast."

"And?"

"Tuthmose has made up his mind. I'm afraid."

"He did what he did for all of us, even you had expressed that you hated her and that if you could you would put '*a dagger in her heart*'

"Words, words, words, no more than that."

He could see that his efforts were futile and wondered if such appeals to the new pharaoh would also be useless. He would try.

And he did to no avail. The temple priests were brought into the matter. Again to no avail.

And Neti, cousin, long time friend of Menes, conspiritor for the new pharaoh, a self proclaimed patriot, a general in the military was never seen again. Menes was unable to persuade the in-coming pharaoh to spare his life The pharaoh who elevated the palace guard to general in the military, never doubted his loyalty refused to intercede on the grounds that it was a bad precedent.

Thus began the long and successul reign of Tuthmose III

CHAPTER THIRTY-SIX

The dream that Tuthmose III had since he was a small boy would now become possible. It would not just be the case of Upper and Lower Egypt but of an empire which would span the Great Sea and points beyond. History books would later call him the Napoleon of Egypt.

Hatshepsut had only reluctantly agreed to any extension of Egypt's borders and now he doesn't have to face further objections from her. As it was, she had lately approved further expansionistic movements and preparations for these were being made at the time of her death.

He had waited twenty-two years to become pharaoh, although the first few years he was not entirely aware that it was his destiny, and as soon as he was able to comprehend this his mother, Isis, had been grooming him for the position. She was the *vizier* in a yet to be recognized court. As far as she was concerned her son, not Hatshepsut, should be pharaoh when his father, Tuthmose II, died. In her mind, and the minds of many others, *she, Hatshepsut,* was the co-regent to him, not the reverse as it later turned out.

And as Tuthmose paused and thought about it, what had she accomplished during the period of her reign? Much. Egypt had been peaceful and prosperous during this era, there had been no major wars and only minor battles as the result of the incursions into Canaan. Many foreigners had volunteered 'slavery' to find a better life in Egypt even as chattels.

But this was not enough for the young pharaoh. He needed to create even a greater Egypt through war and conquest. He truly felt that potential enemies lurked at all of its borders and he needed to display Egypt's power to keep all at a safe distance.

So, he decided to launch many campaigns, wars, to keep those unwanted at a distance and to acquire more wealth and at the same time make Egypt's borders more secure. What he didn't know at that moment was that the Egyptian garrison left earlier in Megiddo, after his successful campaign there, was annhilated by the Canaanites, in revolt, assisted by the Mitanni led by their king Shaushatar. A few Egyptian stragglers, who were able to escape brought the bad news back to the new pharaoh. It was exactly as he had predicted and as he now felt justified in his expansionistic plans.

Prior to Hatshepsut's death, he had assembled a large force in preparation for some movement to the disputed areas, He now doubled this, using propagandas as had his predecessor done, and the volunteers were amassed quickly. Soon he had a standing army of many thousands,

Two Pharoahs

estimated at over 40,000, and the necessary chariots, as well a long boats which would be carried by men to their areas of debarkation. If it was a battle they wanted he would accommodate them with the largest and best trained and equipped military force in the history of Egypt and maybe the world. This time, as before, he would lead his troops to their ultimate destination, he would have to first take and claim the lightly fortified port fortress at Tjaru, establish an Egyptian garrison there, then proceed to the loyal city of Gaza where the 40,000 man army could have a day's rest.

The importance of Megiddo was due to its location. The city was located along the southwestern edge of the Jezeel Valley just beyond Mount Carmel and the Great Sea. At this point Megiddo controlled the trade routes from Egypt to the Mitanni kingdom.

Again, Tuthmose ignored the advice of his commanders, and took his troops through a narrow valley, the short route he insisted and prevailed. The commanders felt that if their troops were narrowed down they would be slaughtered by the waiting enemy as they exited the narrow valley. But he had sent scouts ahead and they reconnoitered and determined that the bulk of the defenders were waiting at the alternative routes. The Egyptians exited the valley onto the plain of Esdraelon between the Canaanites and Megiddo and attacked the Canaanites. The outmanned forces were forced to flee to the fortress at Megiddo. Again, he was correct, or lucky.

En route to their ultimate destination, they took the lightly fortified city of Aruna which gave the Egyptians a clear and open path to their target, Megiddo.

Philip R. Clark

The Egyptians took the lightly fortified areas leading up to the fortress with ease, and both the King of Megiddo and the Mitanni king Kadesh in advance of the Egyptian horde took cover within the city and ultimarely within the fortress. The Egyptian attack which at first used the thousands of bowsmen who rained the copper tipped arrows upon the unsuspecting populace and laid siege that did not last as long as the prior one had which lasted for eight months before. The heroic but vastly outmanned defenders, eventually fell to the Egyptians.

Another king, an ally to the deposed kings, Shaushatar, in turn mounted an inept counter-attack with a vastly outnumbered and inexperienced Matanni army only to be easily defeated. The three kings were then required to each send a son to the Egyptian court for education where they would be taught and required to learn all manners, Egyptian, so they in turn would lead in the sea change in the attitudes toward Egyptian.

In all, they took over 330 prisoners, all military. 26,000 assorted animals, over 800 chariots, assorted weaponry all of which went back to Egypt. Megiddo was re-established as within the Egyptian enclave

The populace was spared.

CHAPTER THIRTY-SEVEN

Tuthmose victoiously returned to Memphis and the financial impact of the 'tribute' and the results of the massive plundering, compensating even the lowliest of the military in ways only imagined by them, brought great wealth to Egypt. And when it came time to start another campaign the ranks were plentiful, eager and ready.

To support this massive build-up he had to find ways to utilize them. To do this, he set about planning his next campign.. His intentions were to solidify his control over Canaan and then into Syria. He correctly estimated that neither would be as easy as Megiddo, as difficult and as long as it was.

Those campaigns took almost two years, including the conversion of territorial hegemony. The populace seemed, in large part , to accept the Egyptians, primarily because their obvious technical superiosity. This may not be the case in the next set of events.

The government that his predecessor had put in place before her untimely death proved to be one important hallmark in her reign. His almost two year absence had little adverse effect on the government and the way it functioned.

There were things of a personal nature that were happening while he was off in battle. His minorwife, Merytra-Hatshepsut, pregnant when he left, had delivered a son and an heir, whom they named Amentohep II, a fit name for a future pharaoh. Nefeure, Hatshepsut's daughter who was also married to Tuthmose III had passed away shortly after her monther's death.

The next two years were spent on Canaan and southern Syria, for the most part collecting 'tributes', paid basically to avoid any further military incursions from Tuthmose's growing army. Growing, because many of the local populations surprisingly swore fealty to the pharaoh and some even joined the Egyptian military, which in lots of cases improved their indivual lives.

Hope did not spring eternal for the Syrians and the Egyptians.

His army replenished both in personnel and the items necessary supplies to wage an extended campaign. Multipile charioteers were trained in the art of driving their chariots while using a bow and arrow against an enemy. Foot soldiers, carrying an assortment of weapons, including swords, spears, maces, cudgels, daggers and bows and arrows honed their skills to the maximum. Boats were built, intended to be carried by lightly armed men trained for this purpose.

Two Pharoahs

Tuthmose III, reviewing his troops, felt that they were more than capable to take on any foe. But which one or ones. He decided to start with the Phoenician cities in Syria. He had sent smaller contingents to collect 'tributes' from the various Phoenician entities as agreed, but noticed a hesitancy on the part of the Syrians. Hence a desire to resolve that matter first.

Then he would take on the wily Kadesh, which would then find him on the banks of the Euphrates. After that he would move west along the banks of the Great Sea. Finally he would consolidate their hegemony in Nubia. That way he would have a consolidared Egypt, from the Euphrated to Nubia and on the north to Syria, having surrounded the country with ones either allied or under Egyptian control. A long hoped for dream, a dream yet to be realized, one that he had tried to persuade his predecessor, Hatshepsut, to move on, but she had vetoed, most times without givng it any consideration. He had felt that a secure Egypt should be surrounded by allies or dependant provinces..She had felt that expeditions into the Land of Punt and Nubia would suffice and at the same time satisfy his empire building passion. Well, she was now dead and he was now the pharaoh and decisions relative to the matter were now undisputably his responsibility. He had little trouble making the necessary decisions. He was now pharaoh. And the pharaoh was an absolute ruler.

And he mused about how the power now accrued to him and he smiled. And then he remembered how Menes had sought, futilely, to have an audience with him about Neti, and how he had distanced himself from the man and he smiled to himself again. "I must find something for Menes to do. Take his mind off his disappointments, something which has already been resolved and something he can't have changed, anyway. Something risky."

CHAPTER THIRTY-EIGHT

Tuthmose's plans decided, he set in motion the largest Egyptian force to that time in quest of his dream of an empire. He moved his forces ahead and surprised the Syrian garrison at Tunip, overwhelming it quickly with minimal casualties. One the walls had been breeched, his expert charioteers quickly overran the city within the walls.

The same applied to Ardata, which fell easily and a jubilant Tuthmose could see his dream unfolding in front of him. He rewarded his troops with a much deserved rest as he planned further campaigns. He was thankful that his casualties had been light and that only a minimum number of replacement would be required.

Instead of open plundering, as had been the rule in the past, regular supply lines were set up between where they were, Ardata, and Egypt, requiring a short span of distance to cover over water. As supplies and troops were built up, Tuthmose sat down with his most seasoned commanders and advisors,and essentially determined the strategy for his next moves.

His grand plan for Syria was to assemble enough troops for a naval assault on the port city of Byblos, thereby bypassing all of Canaan. Days were spent in hastily building long boats to go with those they carried with them, making them a formidable force with which to carry on the attack.Few if any such attacks by sea had been accomplished by now, only those piratical raids which were swift and achieving some specific goal, ie: loot and slaves. So in the dark of night and before the inhabitants were made aware of it, they had overwhelmned the light garrison and had taken over the small city. The Egyptians plundered the city and took a number of captives, some of which were destined for Egypt to work as slaves.

A foothold had been established, now was the time to look toward Dimasqu, the center of the Syrian government. They proceeded north in the Jordan River valley

In their path lay the Kadesh lands which they pillaged with ease laying each small community to waste. There was little resistance to the hundreds of Egyptian charioteers with the accurate bowsmen. All were easily trampled by the savage attacks. They took Simyra and settled in to take stock of their accomplishments before advancing to their ultimate goal.

Dimasqu turned out to be relatively easy compared other cities in the region. The population even seemed to welcome the inevitable. The Egyptians had garnered most of the area's wheat production and sent most of it back to Egyptians leaving most of Syria impoverished.

The population of Dimasqu felt that their conquerors may even show some compassion and were so rewarded.

Word came that there was a rebel uprising back in Ardata, which Tuthmose and one of his commanders, Menes, retuned to put down the uprising. Menes obediently moved into a command position, in the middle of the hostilities and an enemy was able to break through and planted a spear into the man's chest. Menes was able to roll over and pull the spear out and looked to his leader for some assistance or comfort only to have Tuthmose look at him for a short period of time before turning away. He will have to tell his mother and his half brother how brave Menes had been. He will have to order a stele to commemorate the occasion. Taking a spear that was probably intended for him. There was a faint smile on his face. The uprising was handled with extreme severity with most of the males in the town killed or executed.

Tuthmose III returned to the bulk of his body of men and with him the son of the king of Ardata as a hostage to assure the compliance of the Ardata residents as well as their sworn fealty by the king to Tuthmose III, the pharaoh of Egypt. Further he explained in great detail how his 'loyal' general Menes had offered his life sparing Tuthmose's who was the intended victim by slashing the would be assasin with his sword, just as the spear was being thrust at Tuthmose, placing himself between the assassin and the pharaoh and taking the spear himself.

"I have commissioned a stele to commemorate his bravery."

As he and his forces moved west and north , Tuthmose found that to keep the various populations under control, he would take hostages, mostly the sons of nobles thereby under their pain of death, or worse yet slavery, almost guaranteeing their submission.

CHAPTER THIRTY-NINE

After a two year long canpaign a victorious Tuthmose returned to Memphis to find that his primary wife Merytra-Hatshepsut was ill and had been for quite some time. She was being treated and medicated by physicians and was at this point almost well. She had a siege of some malady which caused her be extremely hot and have moments when she was delerious, unable to communicate. Atttendants continually washed her body with cool water and gave her potions of a medicine which came from the bark of trees and commonly used by people from the Land of Punt. The fever subsided, only to come back again in a few days. She complained that before an attack she became very hot, her head felt like it was on fire and ached, as did her bones, her joints and down her back in particular.

He then decided to visit one of his minor wives, Amisi, of whom he had become quite fond. He had found her to be quite urgent and capable of meeting his needs without prompting. To his surprise she already was quite pregnant, about seven months she explained.

He lashed out at her for violating her vow to him and no other and demanded to know the identity of the man involved. When she refused to tell him, he struck her and forced her to the floor, whereupon a young palace guard who had decided to be there, but not visible, stepped forward and asked the pharaoh to stop all the time admitting his involvement. Tuthmose looked at the man, contempt on his face, he strode up and struck the man also driving him to the ground. He then signaled for two more guards "See that this man gets ten lashes and confine him until he joins the next mission across the desert to the east." Accidentally divulging his next campaign plan

"What is your name, guard?" He asked the bound man, now being retained by two others.

"Meti, my lord."

"We'll see each other again" an ominous sound to his voice,. "Take him away, and make it twelve lashes instead of ten."

"And you" as he turned back to Amisi "you are to leave the palace immediately."

"But, where, where?" She had lived in the palace since birth, being the daughter of one the lesser nobles.

He turned on his heels and walked away without answering.

Two Pharoahs

Within a short time two palace guards came to her quarters to make sure she was ready to be escorted out of the palace.

The pregnant Amisi left and was never seen again after that incident.

CHAPTER FORTY

The next campaign was again to Syria whereby he consolidated Egyptian holdings, then turned east to confront the Mitanni. Heretofore his contacts with the Mitanni had been mostly cursory of nature. But to do this he had to cross the Euphrates. His plan was to take his army into Bylbos, now Egyptian, again and build an adequate number of boats to supplement those he had and move overland to Aleppo. And while in Aleppo he would be able to use the hillside trees to still build additional long boats. Then it would be a relatively simple task to carry the boats downhill to the Euphrates.

Along the way to Aleppo and the way down to the river they were able to take many small ungarrisoned cities, pillaging them, and enriching themselves enormously, leaving desolation behind. It was their intent to make sure that word of their advance not get over to the Mitanni.

The Egyptians swept across the river and completely surprised the Mitannian king. Thutmose's quickly routed the Mitanni, a Hurrian country with an Indo-

Two Pharoahs

Aryan ruling class, overwhelming them and seizing their main bases and killing or taking captive a number of the Mitanni. They were able use their own boats to mount a counter-attack, but the well trained and experiences troops were too much for them and the Mitanni were slaughtered.

The Mitanni tried once more to organize a militia and offer some resistance to no avail, as they, too, were no match for Tuthmose's well trained army. With that Tuthmose decided to return to Egypt with the immense booty seized during his numerous raids upon Mitanni cities.

But not for long, his Egyptian garrisons were being periodically attacked by the Shasu, a nomadic people who inhabited, ungoverned, the areas of Lebanon and TransJordan.. It was difficult to either locate or defeat them, leaving only one option that to reinforce each garrison to enable them to handle the problems as they arose.

Gone but not forgotten, the Mitanni rose like phoenix rose from the ashes and spread revolt through the major cities of Syria bringing the Egyptian forces back en masse and thoroughly defeated all of these revolutionary forces

CHAPTER FORTY-ONE

Upon his return to Egypt, he was surprised by the adulation that had developed over the now deceased pharaoh, Hatshepsut. His receptions upon his return were at best tepid. Instead a great deal of attention was being paid to the image of his predecessor. Previously damaged stelae and monuments had been repaired and some additional ones had been completed. The whole matter, a surprise at first, began to infuriate him.

"What did she ever accomplish?" he asked himself, "trees from Punt. Trade missions upon trade missions while we are being threatened from all sides," an obvious exaggeration on his part. And the more he saw the angrier he got. And then he thought about her mortuary temple in the Valley of the Kings and a course of action came to him, but would he be daring enough to actually do it.

He called his vizier and confronted him with the idea. The vizier was shocked that he would want to do anything so ignoble and immediately became concerned with his

Two Pharoahs

own afterlife as well as that of the pharaoh making such a preposterous request.

"There are things which not even a pharaoh should want or even suggest. As is written on her tomb '*O ye who live and exist, who like life and hate death, whosoever shall pass this tomb, as ye love life and hate death, so you offer to me what life you have in your hands, and---*'"

"That's enough," interrupted Tuthmose, somewhat impatient "I'll tend to the matter myself."

And he did, talking to some of less savory troops, he found some rogue Nubians, as it would be difficult, if not impossible to get Egyptians to do what he desired. He was able to convey the message of what he wanted done; Whoever decided to do the act should follow explicit instructions. They were to go to the Hatshepsut's mortuary tomb at Deir el-Bahri, in the Valley of the Kings and remove her mummy as well as four canopic urns and do the same for Senemut, entombed next to her and put them both in a hole in the ground far from her tomb site, where they will never be found Sure that this act would keep her soul from joining her remains in the hereafter. Punishment enough, he thought. For what?? He mused. Depriving him of the throne for as long as she did .Not revenge, no punishment. "You will be rewarded by taking all of the jewelry that has been placed in their mausoleums. If word of this should get out, fear for your lifes."

In addition to those succint orders that were given to destroy or damage any statuary, monuments or stelae

Philip R. Clark

commissioned explicitly by her, excluding the tall obelisks at the entrance to the valley.

That night he explained to his wife what he had ordered and was met with unexpected affrontry, "You should not have ordered that. To defile her image and her tomb" she could not bring herself to call it her 'mummy' "--is not right. Not like a pharaoh. So, why? She was a good pharaoh, a good ruler, and she reigned over a peaceful Egypt." With the emphasis on the 'peaceful'.

"I am building an empire, maybe the greatest ever. That should be sufficient to deter any naysayers."

"You need to talk to the mothers, wives and sisters of your soldiers and maybe you will undersand."

Tuthmose III became quiet as he listened to his wife.

"She was a great builder, in spite of her shortcomings. She kept people working, artisans and slaves alike. Look around you and you can see some of the great things that have been built during her time. Perhaps you should emulate her on those things and maybe we will see more of each other. To say nothing of the education only you can give Amenhotep."

"But she came to the throne in a somewhat illegitmate manner, shoving my father aside, chanting those proverbial sayings about the divinity of her being, when we knew she was only human, human enough to conspire with that Senenmut to render my father helpless and he had to seek relief from my mother Isis."

Two Pharoahs

"False, false, false. Your father was a weak man and his father, Tuthmose, your namesake, could see it from the very beginning and trained her as a prince, leaving your father to wonder about things while he schooled Hatshepsut in the more relavent ways of governance,"

"Things? What things?"

"Things like Isis, your mother, his skin conditions, why it wouldn't go away. His jealousy of his sister/wife. It must have been indicative to all when Tuthmose I, your grandfather, appointed her co-regent to your father and when he had them married. He was thinking of the continuation of the dynasty and felt it had a better chance through her. When he made these decisions you were a dream, a figment of his imagination. And where did he go to get a son, Isis, a minor wife and not of royal blood, which Hatshepsut was, being the daughter of Ahmose and Tuthmose I."

He bristled and went over to her in a menacing gesture, but she stood her ground "You may be right." And turned away.

Yes, the years had passed quickly, and his son and future heir, Amenhotep, was fully grown, and unfortunately reminded him of himself in earlier years, impatient, ambitious and full of ideas which he was anxious to implement. He could see it in his eyes. He recognized that character flaw as one he probably inherited from him. But how? He hardly knew the boy, having been away so much. Empire building. "I must watch that he doesn't align himself with conspiritors who are looking for a change. But he is my son. And I barely know him, and he, I"

ADDENDUM

When we think of Egypt, some of us automatically think of pyramids, sphinx, mummies and the mysticism related to the things that existed there thousands of years ago. Pharaoh Tuthmose, all of them, lived and ruled Egypt during the Eighteenth Dynasty, some thirty five hundred years sgo. Egypt as a society and civilization was ahead of the curve when it came to nearby contemporaries. The period was in the years of the greatest expansion of Egypt, where the 'empire' stretched across North Africa to include present Libya east to Mesopotamia (Iraq) and south to the Fourth Cataract of the Nile. That doesn't mean or infer that other such civilizations didn't exist, as they did , some of them dating back another three to four thousand years before Egypt's zenith.

Hatshepsut was truly a pharaoh and did wonderful things, instituting unbelievable monuments, many of which exist to the day. Her time on the throne in Egypt were peaceful and prosperous.

The acrimony which existed between her and Tuthmose III was real and the level was bitter as he felt that as the son of a pharaoh, Tuthmose II, he not she should be the annointed ruler. It did not happen that way and her father, Tuthmose I, saw that she was talented enough to rule, so he raised her as a 'prince' rather than a princess.

What eventually happened to her is part of my story, however she was mummified, but her mummy disappeared and was claimed to have been found in the nineteenth century. However the claim is suspect. As for the situation with regard to Senenmut, her lover, his mummy has not been found.

Tuthmose III, the 'Napoleon of Egypt' spread Egyptian influence over a wide area as mentioned above. He also captured over 350 cities during his seventeen campaigbs, covering almost a half a century subjugating millions in the process. The Egyptians revered him as a god, as they did all pharaohs.

One last item: "Tuthmose", the *name* as found in history books is spelled in various ways, ie;

Tuthmose, Thuthmose and Thuthmosis. I elected to use the first form.

The author.

ABOUT THE AUTHOR

Born: September 17, 1923

Education: St. Thomas College (High School) Houston, Texas 1940

                    St. Mary's University 1940-41 San Antonio, Texas

                    U.C.L.A. Los Angeles, California 1947-1948

                    University of Southern California, Los Angeles 1948-1951

Service   United States Marine Corps 1941-1945

Personal   Married to wife, Nancy since 1951

                    Three daughters, six granschildren, five greatgrandchildren

OTHER NOVELS BY AUTHOR

PIT STOP

UNCOVENTIONAL CONVENTON

SEPTEMBER SOUND

BENEATH THE BRICKER BARN

FOUR HANDRED AND THIRTY DAYS

STARPOWER

MARK AND ANNE

THE CHAMELEON

All availeble through AUTHORHOUSE
www.authorhouse.com

Printed in Great Britain
by Amazon.co.uk, Ltd.,
Marston Gate.